JANET HUMPHREY

Dust

Book One

First published by Ducklet Publishing 2023

First edition

ISBN: 978-1-7392795-2-3

Editing by nikkib89
Cover art by Kunj Parekh

This book was professionally typeset on Reedsy.
Find out more at reedsy.com

Dedicated to my family & friends who have supported and encouraged me, and my favourite author Iain Rob Wright who inspired me to "Keep going!"

"the researchers figured out that the actual amount of dust falling to the earth is along the lines of 60 tons per day"

Contents

Preface

I started writing this book, inspired whilst on a weekend break in Exeter. I watched a gang of Parkour jumpers at the top of a car park who were leaping over pedestrian's heads from one concrete layer to another.

I wondered what would happen if one of them fell on their heads but didn't die.

My next inspiration was an article from PBS that sixty tons of cosmic dust fall onto the earth every day and that all life on earth is made from cosmic dust.

* * *

Acknowledgement

I have to start by thanking my husband David. Despite not being a fan of fiction he was as important to this book getting done as I was and gave a scientific perspective of the storyline which helped shape the book. Thank you so much for the cups of tea, cuddles, and belief in me. x

My father Stan installed a love of reading and writing in me from a very early age. He won my Senior school's parent's English Writing contest two years in a row (he was then excluded from entering in further years, but I'm sure he would have continued to win !) I owe him so much and hope that this official recognition will make him proud and smile.

To my wonderful mum Valerie, my brothers David and James, and the rest of my lovely family and friends, thank you all for being you.

And finally to my beta readers Aidan, Jodie, Valerie and Stan, and Nikki89 my editor - without your input and enthusiasm for this book, I couldn't have got this far.

1

Dust

Sixty tons of cosmic dust fall on the earth every day

What would happen if some of it was more intelligent than us?

What if it wanted to live, even if you were dying?

Jed, Ezake, Cheri, Samir, Marilyn, Barry, Joshua & Brian

Eight people connected by a unique event

DUST...You cant die whatever happens...it won't let you

2

Arrival

Topsham Road, Exeter

Cathy exits the hospital at the end of her shift as a cleaner. Working long shifts was something she had never really got used to, but after being made redundant from her last job, she had decided not to be choosy.

Three years ago Cathy was a civil servant in a government quango near Exeter, working in the admin department. Unfortunately, despite being assured that the looming cutbacks wouldn't affect her department, that was sadly not true in the end. With a mortgage to pay for, she had applied for the cleaning job, and to her surprise, she was offered the job as supervisor to the team who looked after the hospital. Cathy learned how hard these jobs really were, and in the months following the pandemic, she really appreciated the hard work of her team.

She waves goodbye to her colleagues Anika and Margarita, and she walks to the staff only car park. She is dressed sensibly for her journey home. No boring small car for her - there in the far end of the car park is her brand new 125cc scooter 'Monty'. She smiles every time she sees him.

Her parents thought this was some sort of middle-aged crisis, but as she tried to explain, getting around Exeter in a car is becoming more and more difficult. Riding a scooter is more economical and lots of fun, though she didn't add that to her 'reasons why a scooter is a good idea for me'. Despite being 52 years old, her parents still worry about her, and she decided that the practical reasons why should be at the top of the list rather than the fun parts.

Stopping next to her bike, she puts her handbag and lunch box in the shiny retro top box fixed to the back of the scooter and retrieves her helmet, and puts it on. Although Monty isn't an Italian make, his shiny blue paint attracts lots of admiring glances, and she loves him.

She zips up her jacket, padded and secure, then sits on the saddle whilst she adjusts her gloves so the chilly night doesn't make her hands numb as she rides. Once she is ready, she turns the key in the ignition and she is off on another adventure, or in this case, just going home via the chippy near the hospital for a sausage and chip supper. Cathy smiles as she twists the accelerator

...this is such fun...

She pauses at the T junction to the main road and indicates right to head into the city. She checks her rearview mirrors and is momentarily distracted by a bright flash off to her rear left over the tops of the tree line. She shakes herself mentally reminding herself not to forget her motorcycle trainer's words...

"Always make sure you concentrate on what the other road users are doing and what you need to do to stay alive."

As she accelerates away down the road, she forgets about the flash and ruminates on how quickly she can ride back with her supper in the top box, and whether she can treat herself to a nice glass of wine with her supper.

...It's probably a jet coming into land at Exeter airport...lucky getting away on holiday, though she wouldn't envy them the hassle of quarantine after a nice trip to Spain or wherever...

The flash of light dips below the treeline and smashes into a small glade adjacent to the nearby golf course. Dust fills the air as it disintegrates into small chunks of pebbles and dust. The chunks of pebbles are half-buried in the soft soil, the dust swirls and sparkles in the wind generated from the traffic passing on the main road just beyond the treeline and settles down as each car passes.

During the next few hours in the strengthening wind more, dust particles float down to earth settling in and around the city. The dust sparkles and swirls as people walk through it, and traffic drives over it. Yet no one notices anything unusual; it's just dust.

* * *

ARRIVAL

3

Sarah

A38 Devon Highway

Sarah Matthews wishes for some peace but there was no hope for that with her little geek brother Thomas in the car.

Sitting in the back of her mum's old Ford Fiesta didn't help either, it made more worrying noises every time she had a ride in it, but she knew her mum could barely afford to keep the car on the road. Their mum collected them from school every day and the mileometer on the car was hitting over 100,000 miles. Sarah knew enough about cars that this one was on its last few months.

Thomas piped up again.

"Sis, did you know that 25,000,000 meteoroids weighing 15,000 tonnes hit the earth every single day?" he asked as he consulted his book again. Space science was his favourite subject in the world at the moment. Last month it was rockets after seeing a commercial rocket's successful docking with the ISS on TV.

Sarah smiles despite herself. "No, I didn't know that, Thomas, but how do you know if that is correct? Do scientists get up with big scales to weigh them all?"

He giggles. "No, silly, it's es-tim-ated." That was his new favourite word; he used it for everything from what time he would get to school, how long he would take to eat his dinner, to how long he spent in the bathroom, though Sarah could definitely do without the commentary through the door on what number his "number twos" were on the Bristol Stool Scale. Far too much information.

Their mum was looking more tired today, Sarah mused. Two jobs working to keep them in food and clothes thanks to their feckless dad Jonny refusing to pass over a decent amount in child support, yet he was quite happy to play the dad when it suited him. Especially now when he has a broody hot new girlfriend Cloie...

Sarah wondered often what her mum ever saw in her dad. She dared to ask her once but just got a stern look, so she never tried again. She thought adults were gross most of the time, but watching her dad flirt with Cloie had made her feel sick. Cloie was only ten years older than Sarah and nearly twenty years younger than her dad.

The car continues down the A38 towards Exeter, and Sarah tunes out Thomas's continuing commentary about his new favourite subject.

On the radio, the DJ announces the next track. "In our summer of hits, the next tune coming up is the fabulous Erasure with their chart topping hit – Star."

Sarah's mum Lynne sang along to the tune. Sarah was glad to see a smile on her mum's face now.

As they approach the turn-off, Sarah can see a council road repair truck in front of them, filled with asphalt and sand, also turning off on the same slip road. Lynne slows down and the steering jerks slightly in her hands.

"Bloody workmen," Lynne says, "dropped a load of mess ahead." The car bumps slightly like going over gravel on an off road track, then settles down again.

Sarah joins her mum in singing along to the track on the radio, and Thomas continues to pore over his new book. Life goes on around them, the dust swirls and sparkles slightly in the sunlight and then settles again to wait for more passing traffic....

* * *

4

Jed

Cathedral Green, Exeter

Jed Long steps out of the alleyway into the Cathedral Green and blinks in the strong sunlight. His mind tries to remember what the last few hours consisted of, but his brain is not working well. The large amount of drugs he'd used over the last ten years didn't help. He is tall and skinny, and smells bad, and as pedestrians approach him, they do a little diversion around him, watching him as they pass. He wasn't a bad man, just lost.

Jed had come from an abusive family situation as the social worker kept telling him. His mother had done her best but really being sixteen and knocked up by the local neighbourhood drunk wouldn't have given her the best start in life. His dad had never seen him as far as he knew. Just a squirt and he was gone. His mum had tried hard, but her own habit and getting jailed for shoplifting and prostitution didn't help him.

Eventually, when Jed was aged four and a half he was finally placed in the care of the local social workers. As was normal at the time, the social workers had placed him in a church run children's home when his mum went into hospital. This home had recently been the subject of an expose on local TV. The reporter had gone undercover and found out that widespread abuse and neglect had been normal for the poor children allocated there, and the social workers had given up on them too.

When Jed was ten, he had run away to London to seek his fortune and escape the physical abuse of the home's manager Charlie Gibbons. The home had called the police, and less than forty-eight hours later, he was back. He then tried again multiple times before he realised he needed help. He'd made friends with some of the squatters in an London squat and moved in with them. He knew they would protect him, and after a limited effort, the police and authorities had given up trying to find him.

Since then his family had consisted of those the authorities would have labelled troubled and in some cases mentally ill. Kitty was one of those. She claimed to be twenty, but Jed thought she was nearer seventeen but smart and sassy. She was barely five feet tall, wore her blonde hair in dreadlocks, and dressed like a tramp in charity clothes that didn't match. This style had made her a target for the local university groups that wandered the city after dark. One of them decided in a fit of pique to abuse her from across the road. Kitty ran across and started to beat on the lad's head and body, fiercely muttering as she did.

Only the combined strength of his rugby playing mates kept him from ending up in hospital. Jed witnessed one of them ripping Kitty off his friend, and throwing her to the ground, where she immediately leapt up and tried to attack the lad again. In the end, three of them had been forced to manhandle her back across the road, and dump her at Jed's feet growling that

"if she came back over we would have to kick her arse."

Jed picked Kitty up and managed to drag her away down the road but that was not the last time he would save her from herself. Kitty had a terrible temper and was spoiling for a fight most of the time. She was an angry soul, Jed had told her, yet with him, she was fragile and loving.

Jed staggered over to the bench in Cathedral Green and sat down heavily. He looked up and tried to work out what time of day it was. He also wasn't too sure what day it was. He looked around him, not many tourists, but then they hadn't come back yet. Tourism around Exeter wasn't great even now. One or two groups of tourists huddled near to the Cathedral entrance, a tall gentleman who appeared to be a guide pointing up at the various features. Jed looked around

...mostly work people...

he thought. So probably not the weekend then?

Shielding his eyes he looked skywards.

...Sun was very high so probably middle of the day....

Checking his jacket he pulled out a small sachet with white powder in it. Jed was puzzled as he didn't normally have a stash, as soon as he managed to score, it was gone. He examined the sachet again but discreetly as a few pedestrians were walking by.

...No, didn't look like his normal. Then the clouds confusing his brain started to clear a bit. Mr C!..

Now he remembered.

Mr C had come to the squat to talk to him. Jed was always very afraid of Mr C, and with good reason. His reputation as the hardest man in the South West wasn't a lie. Jed had known a few stupid people who had tried to sucker Mr C or his team, and in all cases, they were either dead or wished they were.

Jed and Kitty had been in bed when the thug had battered down the front door of their squat in Gloucester Road. The building had been empty for many years and the roof leaked badly. When the front door had shattered under the combined weight of the two thugs who accompanied Mr C, the dust in the hallway swirled and moved around as they entered.

None of the other squatters had been there, and that was probably a blessing. Jed and Kitty woke with a start as they heard heavy footfall coming down the filthy hallway into the room they had claimed as their own. The door slammed open, Jed had staggered out of the filthy bed and stood trembling as the thug got closer, then moved aside as Mr C followed him in.

Mr C wrinkled his nose at the combined odour of sweat, urine, and a foul stench coming from the bathroom next door. Kitty had curled into a small ball on one of the pillows and was trying not to look at anyone. She whimpered softly and muttered unintelligible things to herself as she rocked gently.

"Jed my man" drawled Mr C, a small natty dressed Turkish national as he approached Jed with a smile that could have come from a great white shark. Mr C was always a very natty dresser and today he seemed to have sparkled with gold around his neck from a heavyweight chain, a linen suit which was probably hand made and stylish highly polished brogues.

"How have you been?"

Jed trembled, even more, his throat was so tight he felt like he couldn't even breathe "F-f-fine Mr C." Mr C came a lot closer to him and smiled even wider.

"Kevin here," he indicated to the thug who had destroyed the front door "suggested I came and chatted to you about a nasty rumour I am hearing about a grass somewhere in my considerable empire. You wouldn't happen to know anything about that would you?"

Jed staggered back and landed sitting on the bed. He looked up pleadingly

"No, Mr C, I'd never, you've been so good to me - the room and all..." Jed trailed off. Mr C sat down next to Jed and placed a meaty manicured hand on his shoulder.

"That's what I said to Kevin, my man Jed would never do me over. He's much more clever than that. That's why I have decided you are going to be my tester for a new batch that has just arrived."

Mr C produced a small sachet and shook it at Jed.

"Here, catch."

Jed stumbled but managed to catch the edge of the packet

"New b-batch Mr C. What is it?"

Mr C smiled broadly and slapped Jed on his shoulder "Fine product, I just need a reliable source to test it for me, and who better than you?"

Mr C stood and brushed down his jacket.

"Let me know what you think - usual way - at the casino OK?"

Jed nodded frantically. "Yes sir. Thank you, Mr C."

Kevin and Mr C left the room and stepped over the shattered front door out into the crisp cold morning air. Jed sunk back onto the bed and his throat finally opened so he could cry out loud. He was pretty sure he'd pissed himself, but that wasn't the worst of it. Kitty had disappeared into the bathroom, and he could hear her sobbing. Jed staggered up to the bathroom door and banged on it.

"Baby - it's OK he's gone, and he's left us a sample." Kitty sobbed louder.

"OK babe, I did offer to share it with you." Jed put the sample into his coat which was thrown onto a chair and fell back onto the bed and within ten minutes he was snoring loudly. Kitty trembled as she opened the bathroom door and then crawled back into bed, but didn't sleep for a long while.

On the bench, Jed examined the sachet again squinting in the brightening sunlight.

That was Sunday, Mr C had visited, and today was Tuesday, right?

"Ay mate - what day is it?" he demanded of the posh woman walking by with her friend. She looked at him with disgust and didn't bother replying.

"Tuesday, my friend," said the bloke who looked like a builder on the next bench to Jed "every day is the same in paradise right?"

Jed nodded and walked off. He was feeling better already. He headed back to the squat expecting Kitty or the others to be there, but no, the place was quiet. The front door had been nailed back into place, it couldn't be opened anymore, but that was probably for the best when the bailiffs came back again.

Jed walked around the side and slid under the construction fence that surrounded the property. He jiggled up the latch on the downstairs window and slid the window up so he could get back in. On the other side, Jed nearly stood in a bucket of sewage placed under the window to deter the bailiffs who had already come three times last week to evict them. So far they had not been successful but Jed was aware it was only a small victory and that he and Kitty would be out on the streets before too long. Mr C had arranged for their room, but he didn't own the building, and the real owners wanted to sell to developers for new flats.

Jed made his way to his bedroom and sat down on a rug on the floor. Taking out the sachet, he saw that there was enough there for him and Kitty. He poured about a third out for her into a cup, then placed the rest of the powder on the table and moved it into two long lines. He didn't like shooting up if he didn't need to, though his nostrils were starting to die off, so he might need to go back to that before long.

Jed bent down and holding one nostril closed, he manoeuvred a soft drink straw along the edge of the powder and sniffed. Immediately, his brain sizzled. The powder Mr C had given him was nearly 90% pure, and it wasn't for his pleasure or high but for Mr C's business. Mr C had recently learned that Jed had been arrested in the city last week for being drunk and disorderly, and on arriving at the Exeter Police station booking in desk, he had proceeded to spill his guts about friends in high places.

Unfortunately for Jed, the young booking clerk was also on Mr C's books due to a long standing gambling problem he didn't want his employers to learn about. He had reported the conversation and the fact that Jed had spent a long time chatting with the drug squad team before being released on bail.

What the booking clerk wasn't aware of was that Jed hadn't been sober enough to talk, so the squad had learned nothing other than what a hard life Jed has, and yet by the end of that day, his cards were marked. Mr C preferred to let people's own bad habits kill them, with a little assistance of course. Just another junkie death.

Jed's eyes rolled back and his breathing stopped. He foamed at the mouth, lost control of his bladder and bowels, but his heart continued to beat normally and he didn't die.

* * *

Three hours later the bailiffs finally managed to batter their way into the property and found Jed slumped on the floor near the table. The senior bailiff stepped outside to call the police and ambulance after establishing that Jed was not dead. Jed's troubles were only just beginning.

On arrival, the motorbike paramedic had thought that this case could be an overdose of fentanyl but the symptoms he observed didn't match those. There was no breathing, a normal heart beat and this patient's skin wasn't cold and clammy but warm and normal. If it wasn't for the breathing, this patient would be transported to hospital to sleep off whatever he had taken.

The paramedic called for an ambulance to take the patient for an assessment, and when the ambulance team arrived, the motorbike paramedic logged off the call and was allocated back to the roving team again. The ambulance team monitored Jed's reactions and his lack of breathing with some trepidation wondering out loud if a new drug was around they had not heard about.

On arrival at Exeter Hospital, Jed was taken through to the Resus room and was assessed by the trauma team. They were all shocked when they realized that despite Jed not breathing, his heart was beating strongly without assistance from an oxygen tank. None of them had ever seen such a case and they could not explain this anomaly.

The lead Doctor on call decided to contact the team at DHSC, the Government's health department in case this was a new disease they had not so far seen. Jed was placed in isolation, and as was the case with any hospital patients, he was screened for other diseases including COVID, which all came up negative. Jed's heart continued to beat strongly. He did not breathe, he did not die.

* * *

5

Ezake

A38 Devon Highway near Chudleigh

The brand new Volkswagen Golf R accelerated away from the roundabout doing 60 mph in a 40 mph zone. Ezake Mosey smiled as the car changes up gears again. He glanced over to his pretty white hottie sitting in the passenger seat. Cheri was beautiful and she knew it. She liked being the one girl he wouldn't cheat on, despite the temptations of his line of work. She wore a micro mini dress that rode up her slim legs, with heels that she could barely walk in, though she didn't walk much anywhere these days, just sat on the expensive shabby chic chaise lounge in their Quayside apartment, called her friends on video calls and watched Tik Tok videos all day.

Ezake had the Devon route sorted, Mr C, his boss had trusted him as one of his senior couriers but had also warned him that he shouldn't get caught and never grass, or he'd end up like that junkie overdose.

Ezake knew that Mr C has believed Jed had told the Police about some of the operations out of Exeter and that Mr C was responsible for what had happens to him.

...Shame he didn't die...

Ezake thought. Mr C was furious when he found out Jed wasn't dead, but from all reports, he wasn't going to be grassing again ever.

Mr C had lots of rules, don't drive fast, stay within the limits, look like a businessman going home from a boring job, don't cheek the police if you get caught, and most of all, don't get caught.

Ezake smiles at the last rule.

...Yes a courier shouldn't get caught with half a kilo of pure cut cocaine in the car though at first glance it just looked like three cases of the finest Jamaican Rum...

If he was stopped, he had paperwork to show it was being shipped from Mr C's warehouse in Plymouth to an exclusive party being held at a former media star's house to celebrate finishing his latest stint in rehab. No reason for the Devon Traffic Police to realize that taking one swig of any of the bottles in the back of the car, would end their lives.

The journey from Plymouth to Exeter should have taken an hour but roadworks had held them up and he needed to be in Exeter to hand over by 8 pm. He knew that the centre of Exeter had more road works and Mr C's pad above the casino was on the other side of the city.

He pulls out of the slowing line of traffic and accelerates again. He steals a glance over at Cheri who is concentrating on a Tik Tok video on her mobile phone.

"Nearly there, babe," he smiles at her, she barely glances up at him. She looked back down at her phone and smiled at the video she was watching.

As Ezake accelerated again, the wheels became locked and started to slide and he realized too late that there was some sort of substance on the road,

...*Oil !!*

...*Shit...!*

he thinks as he tries to control the car, but the speed and the lack of grip just propels the car and its unfortunate occupants into the treeline just past the turning for Chudleigh.

As the car smashes into the treeline, the car engine is propelled backwards into the driving compartment and cuts off the lower half of Cheri's body and the one arm she held the phone in. The remainder of her torso and head remains upright and she has a slightly puzzled expression on her young face.

The airbag doesn't inflate as the engine entering the compartment cuts the vital wires. Ezake is saved by the steering wheel stopping the engine from cutting him in half, however, their problems have only just started.

Ezake is mercifully unconscious when the fire starts from the petrol igniting and the bottles of rum exploding, the flames licking around the inside of the car.

Cheri's legs, arm, and lower torso slump down into the passenger's footwell as the bottles of doctored rum explode as the heat of the crash reaches them. Ezake and Cheri's agony is compounded by more of the bottles of spirits mixed with cocaine exploding in the fierce heat that now engulfs the car.

Cheri's mouth opens in a scream but nothing comes out of her mouth. Thankfully she is rendered unconscious at this point. Both Ezake and Cheri do not breathe, their hearts beat strongly and neither of them dies.

As the car and the occupants burn, the traffic behind them slows to a stop and people exit their cars. On the opposite carriageway, the traffic also comes to a halt watching the scene with horror.

The first reports reach the 999 call centre in Exeter at 6.32 pm. The first ambulance and patrol car reach the scene of the accident in under four minutes thanks to the public making passing room for their vehicles assisted by the blues and two's on both vehicles.

As the police car draws up, the treeline is ablaze and the Golf R is embedded in one of the trees about four feet up about five hundred feet past the sign for Chudleigh. The other carriageway has slowing traffic, due to the number of gawkers who are watching the fire as they pass in their cars.

"Bloody ghouls" grunts Special Road Crime Officer Martin Phillips as he starts to turn the traffic on the side of the accident down the slip road and onto his colleagues who were setting up a diversion to move the traffic onwards towards Exeter.

His colleague Minty Stafford hops over the central reservation barrier and starts to usher the traffic on the other side along more quickly.

"No point in trying to see if anyone's alive," comments Minty as he waves on more traffic.

"Bloody BBQ up there, no chance for any poor sods," agrees Martin as he waves down the ambulance into the lay by. The paramedics get out, with their grab bags and assess the scene.

"Going to need the fire truck here too to get that blaze out," said the lead paramedic.

"On their way," said Martin, "should be here shortly."

The fire truck pulled up just after he spoke, and the team got out and started to pull a ladder and a hose reel jet across to the treeline and started to extinguish the flames around and inside the car.

"Looks like the car had something flammable other than the fuel," said the Incident Commander. "My Sector Commander suggests that there was booze or something in the back."

Within a short period of time, the flames had been extinguished both from the treeline and also from the car which is now steaming. SRCO Martin Phillips looks across from where he is directing traffic to see his colleague James compiling the collision report.

He thinks

...That's going to be one of the worse crashes this year for the Collisions Team to investigate...

As he continues to direct traffic off at the Chudleigh turn-off, he sees the Collision Investigation Unit car approach the scene.

Thomas McCall his colleague in the Unit gets out. As he approaches Martin, the Fire Team are finishing dampening down the car and the trees and packing up their kit to go. Thomas approaches the car carefully, trying not to slip in the mud that had been created by the vast amounts of water from the fire engine. The senior paramedic looks over from where he is examining what's left of the driver, his face is sheet white.

"This one is alive, God help me," he says.

"What do you mean? How can they be alive," Thomas replies, shocked.

"Don't know guv, but there is a heartbeat, no breathing."

The Paramedic calls over to the Fire team.

"We've got a live one here." They rush over with the jaws of life and proceed to extract the driver carefully from the car. As the paramedic moves the casualty to a stretcher Martin notices that Thomas is on a phone call which is unusual for him, he is normally focused on the scene until he gets back to the office.

The other paramedic is checking the passenger and looks over towards the fire crew

"Another live one," she says with a slightly sickened look on her face. "God knows how"

She looks down into the passenger compartment and on the floor are the remains of a lower torso and legs. Still held in place by the seatbelt, the passenger, barely more than a head, upper torso, and one arm blackened by the intense fire, and with a skull with lips burned away. Only the presence of what would have been diamond earrings, and a single strand of blonde hair suggested that the passenger may have been female once.

Thomas comes over and converses with the paramedics as they load the casualties onto the stretchers and as Martin gets distracted by the traffic still slowing on the other carriageway, he doesn't notice that the ambulance isn't showing its blues and twos and drives off not at the rapid pace they normally do.

When the traffic is back to its normal pace, Martin and Minty get back in their patrol car and log off the scene. As they drive away, Martin asks, "Did you see that those poor sods weren't dead?"

Minty grunts as he looks up. "Aye, God only knows What's going to happen to them. I predict DOA when they get to Exeter"

Minty grunts again and looks at his watch. "Better get a move on Martin me chum - bacon sandwiches won't last long in the canteen and I'm starving."

Martin looks sick - after that call, he doesn't think he could stand crispy meat ever again, and he wonders how Minty could face a slab of bacon after all they saw earlier. As they arrive back at their base station, Martin muses on the fate of the two poor souls in the car.

By the following day, and after several more incidents, he has put them to the back of his mind alongside the other casualties he assists in his job. Less than two weeks later, when the news broke around the world, did Martin realise the case he had attended was one of the ones being cited by the British Prime Minister as being #notdead.

* * *

6

Samir

Samir wiped his face on his t-shirt again.

...This room he's been working in all day is beginning to smell. Or is it me? ..

He sniffs his armpit carefully.

Nope, that's me, he thinks. Not surprising considering how much work I've done already.

He looks back across the room.

...Fifteen boxes of new stock are now on the shelves, just the alcohol to finish up with...

He picks up the next box, six one litre bottles of the Polish vodka his dad's been stocking for a year. The builders working on the new housing estate up the street buy them as soon as they arrive in the store.

Samir's dad owned the convenience store now for over forty years. Despite getting eight grade '9's in his recent exams, Samir knows his dad relies on him to help out in the shop.

"Never going to get to vet school," Samir says out loud.

"Why do you want to put your hand up a cow's bum?" his dad had often asked. "Why can't you be a proper doctor like your cousin Tamir?" The cousin in question now works as a surgeon in Manchester earning the respect of his parents and the wider Muslim community.

Unfortunately, all of his family thought that all vets only put their hands up cows' bums, but he'd given up trying to explain he wanted to be a small animal vet, like his friend Andy wanted to be. Samir's dad refused to let Samir have a pet, even a goldfish, so he had to be content with going to Andy's house to study where there was a multitude of pets: cats, a dog, and also now chickens in the back garden.

Vets don't cut it in Pakistani society, Samir thought. But it's all he ever wanted to do.

As Samir comes back into the shop, he realizes two people have entered since he went back into the storeroom. He didn't hear the bell on the door though.

As he rounds the shelving with the box in his hand, he recognizes one of the people. It was Matty Bartlett, the one person Samir hoped he wouldn't ever have to see again. Matty B, as he liked to be known, was the worst bully at his school, and for some unknown reason, Samir was the one person Matty decided needed his special attention most of all.

Samir hefted the box closer to him and tried to ignore Matty.

"Give us one," mutters Matty. Samir ignores him and continues down the aisle to the alcohol aisle.

As he puts down the heavy box, he realizes who the other person is. It's James Marston, one of Matty's little dogsbodies. Matty had a few, but James is one of the ones Matty seemed to keep. Though after being expelled from their year for pulling the fire alarm, Samir wonders if James's family might try and keep him away from Matty. Samir knew that James was a clever kid, Samir had only beaten him by one grade in their recent exams.

"Give us one," says Matty again, pointing to the box at Samir's feet.

Samir looked up. "No," he said. "My dad will be back soon."

Although it's more likely that he will be late back from the accountant's,

Samir thought. He bent down to open the box and realized Matty had moved closer.

"Give us one or you'll get my fist in your face." Matty sneered. Samir paled as he remembered the last day of school when Matty announced to his gang that this was "bash-a-paki day" with a snigger. Samir still had the bruise on the back of his arm where Matty had repeatedly thumped him.

Samir bent over the box but looked up when he heard a sob. James was standing about four feet away looking white and scared. As Samir stared at him, he realized it too late. Matty had bent even closer and thumped him in the right side, near his ribs.

The pain was enormous, hot, and like a fire in his side. He looked up at Matty, who had a huge grin on his face and a blade in his hand. It was sticky and red.

...Blood thought Samir. That's my blood. Oh God, he stabbed me...

Samir slid to the floor cradling the box of vodka as he slumped, watching Matty saunter off with a bottle in his hand. James looked like he might be sick all over the floor. Matty grabbed James by the arm and the bottle in the other hand and propelled James out as Samir's blood coated the box and the floor. Samir's breathing stops, his heart continues to beat even as his blood spreads across the floor but he doesn't die...

* * *

Two hours later Mr Azmed came back into the shop. He frowned as he expected to see Samir manning the till. "Where is that boy?" he muttered. As he rounded the shelving at the end of the shop, he spotted Samir slumped over a box on the floor.

"Sammi, what's happened?" said Mr Azmed as he rushed down the aisle. As he came closer, he could see Samir's eyes were shut and his face was grey. Mr Azmed pulled out his mobile phone with one hand and shook Samir by the shoulder with the other hand.

Samir slumped to the floor, and at that point, Mr Azmed could see the red stain all across his son's shirt and coating the box of vodka.

SPC Emma Bates arrived at the convenience shop shortly after the 999 call by Mr Azmed. She spotted her friend and colleague Jack Knotsford manning the tape line.

"Hi, Jack. Stabbing, isn't it?" she asked as she came level with the open front door of the shop. She spotted the paramedic crew inside the shop near the alcohol aisle.

Jack looked pale as he nodded. "Yes, the young lad, the son, was stabbed earlier. The medics are working on him, but they are taking their time." Emma looks surprised, normally they stabilize and go. Across the road in another ambulance was Mr Azmed senior, with a blanket around his shoulders, being tended by another ambulance crew. He looks gray and pale. She considers going over there, but just as she was about to, she spots DC Martin Smythe heading over to the ambulance with his note book and pen out ready.

She turns back to see the paramedic crew bringing out Samir. He has an oxygen mask on but the senior paramedic is on the phone with someone which is strange as they are normally closely monitoring their charges.

Emma walks over to her colleague Jack. "What's going on?" she asked.

"No idea," said Jake with a shrug. "But Smythie boy has just got back in his car, I assumed he would be speaking to the father for a good long while"

Emma stares over at the activity at the shop, officers marking out blood spots and footprints in the soft kerbside near to the shop front. She frowns and then turns back to Jake, waving goodbye to him before she sets off on her foot patrol of the local area again.

Samir was loaded onto the ambulance, and it set off towards the hospital. On arrival, however, unlike other emergency cases arriving at A & E, Samir is unloaded and taken towards an unused part of the hospital near to the new mortuary, where on arrival his vital signs are assessed by the trauma team. This team was being assisted by a special task force from DHSC, who had arrived at the hospital after they were alerted to Jed's case.

In the unit also being monitored were Jed, Ezake, and Cheri. Batteries of tests had already been undertaken on all three of them, but no results explaining their state had been suggested. Ezake and Cheri were heavily bandaged, for their burns were extensive and nearly all third degree across the remainder of their bodies. Both Ezake and Cheri had lost limbs in the crash, and their forms in the hospital beds were tragic and traumatic for the teams looking after them. Jed in comparison had a healthy pink glow to his skin, and if it wasn't for the eerie lack of breathing, he would at first glance appear to be a coma patient.

Samir's condition was assessed on arrival, and the medical and science teams were shocked to realize the volume of blood he had lost was much higher than that which would be expected to result in his death by exsanguination. However, he wasn't dead either; none of them were.

* * *

7

Marilyn

Marilyn Francis opens one eye and groans softly.

...That third glass of red wine foisted on to her by her best friend Sue at their Spanish wine and cheese party next door really wasn't such a good idea, but at the time it was delicious...

She tentatively lifts her eye mask, and the sunlight streaming into her bedroom makes her groan again.

She should really know better at her age. She was a sprightly seventy one years old, petite and lean. A widow for fifteen years, she had been married to Jeremy for thirty four years. Thirty four great years for the most part, until he had a heart attack at work sat at his desk at midnight trying to get the accounts sorted out for the local Indian restaurant in town.

He'd been an accountant since birth, his family had said when they met Marilyn. He had been a good husband, a fantastic partner, but children were not part of their lives. Neither Jeremy nor Marilyn had wanted children, which back in the 1970's was not expected. Both sets of parents had desperately wanted grandchildren, but in the end, Marilyn and Jeremy's siblings had provided these, so all was well in the end.

Marilyn and Jeremy had been one of the first couples to travel overseas, and every year their fridge had another magnet from some far off destination added to it. At one point Jeremy had joked that they needed a new fridge, not because anything was wrong with it , but that they had run out of room for their fridge magnet collection. That was their life together, joking and laughter, and plenty of travelling.

She swings her legs over the side of the bed and staggers to her feet. Making her way to her en suite bathroom, she contemplates the day to come.

...COVID Marshall duties at the local civic hall at 2 pm followed by an evening of discussions about the latest book by some popular author in Sue and Keith's garden again....

Marilyn wasn't impressed with the prose or the plotline of the current book but she knows that Sue and Keith wanted to be sociable. She needed to "make an effort" her husband would have said, he was right she knew that she needed to.

Sue and Keith had both been happy to host these events, especially since they were both now double jabbed as Sue kept on mentioning. COVID lockdown had been a very tough time for Marilyn and she was grateful for the company of Sue and Keith, and their kindness. They had made sure that they checked in with her a couple of times a week, standing well back from her front door in the sheltered housing complex they all lived in.

Fifteen spacious bungalows with a warden on hand, at the press of a button, if needed. Marilyn had lived in Munstead Gardens off Paris Street for nearly five years now. She had sold her home in nearby Exminster, and moved into a light and airy bungalow on the north side of the complex. She was lucky that her nephew Jacob had been keen to help her move. He had rallied his university chums and in the end, five strapping lads and Jacob had hired a huge van and got all of her possessions into it, and back out in the new place without breaking anything.

Jacob was a student at Exeter, and often popped in to see his aunt for a cup of tea now she was settled. She worried about him a lot. He was her only relative in the UK. All her other family had emigrated to Canada and New Zealand back in the 1980s. She got letters from them occasionally and sometimes a call, but she was glad Jacob was nearby.

She sighs again and gets washed and dressed. She goes downstairs and turns on the portable radio in the kitchen. Radio 2 comes on and "Kansas - Dust in the Wind" starts to play. As she hums along to the tune, she notices her pedal bin is smelly so she bags up the bin liner and takes it outside to the community bins.

As she turns to go back inside she spots Keith opening his curtains and waves at him.

...He looks worse than I feel...

she chuckles to herself...as he waves back but she can tell his head is hurting as much as hers is.

She staggers on the back step to the kitchen as a wave of enormous dread comes washing over her. She topples backwards onto the path. Her heart pumps hard, her lungs stop working and yet she doesn't die. Keith watches in horror from his kitchen window as his neighbour and friend topples back on the pathway in front of her bungalow.

"Sue, Sue! Something's wrong with Marilyn - press the button woman!"

Keith dashes out of his front door, and over to where Marilyn is lying slumped on the pathway

"Marilyn honey, are you OK?" as he kneels down beside her on the path.

He knew the answer was no, from her grey colour. Sue follows out in her housecoat with her phone in her hand.

"I've called 999 Keith, and pressed the button."

A few minutes later the wardens front door opens up and Lisa, the warden comes out, putting on her cardigan over her nightdress.

"What's happened?"

She spots Marilyn lying on the floor

"I've called 999 Lisa, and they are on their way."

Lisa kneels down and listens for a breath - nothing. She feels for a pulse and is surprised and shocked to find that Marilyn's heart is beating strongly with a good rhythm. Lisa had been the first responder at Munstead Gardens for eight years and she had attended quite a few incidents like this.

She had never come across a situation like this where the person had stopped breathing but their heart was working well. Normally patients had a very fluttery heart rhythm which indicated heart issues. No one noticed that Marilyn's colour had gone from grey back to a healthy pink.

Sue gives rescue breaths until the paramedics arrive three minutes later. Sue and Keith moved off to give them some room. Lisa updated the paramedic team on the condition of Marilyn and was surprised to see one of the paramedics excusing themselves and moving across to the far pathway where they were making a phone call. Quickly returning the paramedic speaks to the other one softly who nods.

"We're taking her now, love," he said.

"Exeter hospital?" asked Keith. "Shall we follow? We're good friends of Marilyn, we have all her details."

Lisa puts a hand onto Keith and says, "No Keith, it's OK. I'll follow her to the hospital. Sharon will be on shift shortly so she can look after you both."

As the paramedics leave with Marilyn on a stretcher, Keith realizes that he didn't get an answer to his question about where they were taking his friend. Keith walks back to his bungalow hand in hand with Sue, to make a call to Marilyn's nephew Jacob.

* * *

Ten minutes later Jacob bursts through the external door leading to the sheltered bungalows.

...*He looked manic*...

thought Keith, as he walked down to meet him.

"Jacob, they've taken her to hospital." Jacob looked frantic, and as he turned, his friend Lee caught hold of him.

"I'll take you mate, come on the car's outside." Jacob waved distractedly at Keith and Sue and walked quickly back outside into the busy street beyond.

* * *

8

Barry

Barry Stephens unlocks the door of the house he has been working on for the last three weeks. Exeter Mansions was a small development on the east side of Exeter near junction 5 of the M5.

...More yuppy mansions...

he scoffs, but as the heritage restoration work he prefers to do was cancelled due to the lockdowns, he has to accept that he might have to do some work he doesn't really want to do these days.

As he enters the downstairs he notices that the living room hasn't had much more work done to it since the last time he was there. Some of the other contractors were from Poland, and a lot of the ones he used to see a lot of, had gone back home during the COVID lockdown. Some of them never came back, finding that work in Poland had improved and they could be closer to their families now.

Barry was fifty four and sturdy, as his mates called him. He was recently divorced from his childhood sweetheart Maisie. Brian and Maisie had met at secondary school in the 1980s and had married aged eighteen. Three kids had followed, but the lack of money during the recession in the 1990s had led to Maisie deciding she had to get a job to help support the family. Despite not having many qualifications, she started working at a local estate agents as a receptionist during school hours.

After three years the branch manager suggested that she start the exams which would lead her to become an estate agent. She aced the exams and after a short while started to earn more money than Barry did. As the dynamics of their relationship changed, Barry got more and more morose about the situation.

Instead of finding pleasure in the skills of his wife and how clever he was to have married her, he derided her, expected her to look after him and the kids as well as full time work. Maisie tried her best but in the end, after many rows she decided to leave. The kids, all boys - Hugo, aged seventeen, Mark aged fifteen and Ryan aged twelve, all now strapping teenagers took his wife's side and moved with her into a small bungalow on the other side of the city. Barry didn't see much of any of them these days.

As Barry climbs the stairs to the first floor, with his bag of tools, he contemplates the day to come.

..Had this bathroom to finish wiring, then it was on to the next one in the block...

As he enters the bathroom, he sees that some of the tilings has been done, but there is a pile of tiles on the floor next to where the toilet, washbasin and sink will be going.

As he lays down his bag, he realizes too late he is standing in the big puddle of water on the floor directly in front of the wall where the wires are sticking out. The electric shock hits him and propels him into the wall behind him. The shock through his body stops his heart briefly then it starts again. His breathing stops, his heart carries on strongly, but he doesn't die.

The noise of Barry collapsing brings the other workmen in the house to see what's happened.

One of them comments as he runs up the stairs to his friend in Polish that the "elektryk has fallen over the tiles in the bathroom." His friend pulls back on his arm saving his life, he's spotted the water on the floor and running down the wall. They both turn away and run to call 999.

Within five minutes the Rapid Response Vehicle (RRV) arrives with paramedic John Steid at the wheel. The Polish workmen show the paramedic where the patient is, and as John climbs the stairs he asks the workmen what the name of the patient is.

They reply "Elektryk" which confuses him until he gets to the landing. He comes back down and asks them where the power is. They point along the wall where the generator is. He switches it off and goes back up the stairs, which are now dark.

He switches on his headlamp and assesses the scene. The patient is lying in a pool of water. John uses a large piece of timber to move the cable on the floor away from the water and approaches his patient. He assesses that he is not breathing and calls command on his walkie talkie to get an ambulance sent for Respiratory arrest.

He checks Barry's pulse and other vital signs and is astonished that Barry appears to have a very strong heartbeat, and the electrical current doesn't appear to have caused the usual dangerous ventricular arrhythmias that would often present after a shock of this nature. Ten minutes later the ambulance crew arrived and transport Barry down the stairs and into the ambulance. The senior paramedic signs John Steid off the scene, and he returns back to the RRV pool for his next assignment.

As the team checks Barry's vital signs, the ambulance speeds towards the hospital. The senior paramedic Mandy Rogers calls for assessment and the ambulance is also diverted back to the DHSC assessment unit. Each of the crews and other medical personnel had been alerted to send patients displaying similar signs to those already observed in Jed, Ezake and Cheri directly to the unit. Mandy and her team unload Barry and take him inside where gowned medical teams were waiting for this latest casualty.

* * *

9

Joshua

Joshua Cooper was seventeen years old. Tall and gawky in stature, he wasn't a confident teen, unlike his mates. He did have a skill that they didn't have. He was a very good video gamer. He made videos mostly about gaming especially his skills on Minecraft, Battlefield, Saint's Row and so on. In front of the camera talking about gameplay and strategy, he was as confident as a chairman of the board. He desperately wished his skills could be used in real life, like for chatting up girls, but no, he stumbled over his words and ended up blushing like a tomato.

Two weeks ago one of his fans suggested that he upload a video of him doing parkour. Joshua wasn't keen on this as he didn't like heights but the fan started a viral hashtag #joshuaparkourchamp which unfortunately gained more momentum than he wanted it to.

Joshua's business manager Sarah Keen then suggested that perhaps he "should give the fans what they want" in their last meeting. Joshua's dad Dave who was a bit of an idiot agreed with her, and here he was on top of a windy car park in Exeter with some parkour experts having some lessons.

Joshua had been introduced to Sarah Keen at one of the gaming expos he had gone to. He had been standing in line to do a meet and greet with one of the top gamers in the industry three years ago, and after shaking hands and having a picture taken, Sarah had tapped him on the shoulder and asked if he was into gaming too. Dave had come over at that point, his dad was quite protective of him, but Sarah hadn't been upset but had thrust out her hand and introduced herself as a manager. Her client was not as well known as the one they were observing but Joshua knew his name. Sarah had passed over her business card to Dave and moved off to allow more fans to pass by.

Several weeks later Dave had come by Joshua's room with the card in his hand.

"I've done some research on this woman we met."

"Oh ay," said Joshua distractedly as he foxed an opponent online.

"Yeah, she's good it seems. She got her client a lot of sponsorship and his channel has gone up in the ratings since she started working for him. Might be worth meeting her. She lives in Exeter apparently." Joshua grunted back which Dave took to mean agreement. The following week, Sarah arrived on their doorstep bright and cheerful despite being soaked in rain during the short walk from the car.

"Good morning Dave, good morning Joshua," she said as Dave beckoned her into their home. Over the next two hours with a cup of tea in her hand, Sarah explained the magic of sponsored posts and partner advertising. She showed them both the approximate figures Joshua could earn for every 1000 clicks to his video blogs and how to make them more appealing. She had done some considerable analysis on his latest three video posts and came up with a lot of great ideas. Dave was impressed with her, but Joshua was unsure. He just liked making the posts. Sarah decided to let the information sink in. She thanked them both for their time and the tea and left them to think about it. She could see that Joshua could be great, really great, but she needed them to need her. That was how she made money herself, but the idea had to appear to have come from them.

It only took twelve hours for Dave to call her back and another five days for formal management of Joshua's career to begin. Sarah was very good at her job and Joshua's ratings started to rise. She had a team of people whom she used for her other clients, who helped Joshua with his content, and advised him on legal issues when the channels started to require talent to declare their sponsored posts more clearly. Joshua didn't have this problem to start with but when gaming console companies started to contact Sarah, things started to change, with promotional gifts of games and consoles for him to review and critique.

Three years on, just because of some supposed fan starting a viral tag, here he was standing on a concrete parking roof, at his most vulnerable.

I hate it, the whole thing parkour.

... hated the height, the ability of the other people, being able to leap from one high point to another and even climb walls without ropes ffs. How can they do that without being Spiderman? Do they have webbed feet?

he looked over the one expert he particularly didn't like - Adam, tall, blonde tanned and with a great fit body wearing baggy grey joggers, a tight fitting black t-shirt and a very expensive pair of trainers. Joshua had worn similar clothing, but he looked like a runner bean dressed up, skinny, weedy even.

He looked over at Sarah Keen and his dad who were in deep conversation with the camera crew they had hired for the day. The wind was getting up again and the rain clouds across the horizon were coming closer. Sarah had persuaded the council that they were shooting a video for his next series, but that was a load of rubbish. Joshua wondered what the council would say if they knew what was actually happening.

Joshua's mum Jane had not wanted to be a mother - Joshua had loved his mum completely, and when his parents had decided to divorce, Jane had given him over to his dad, and Dave had stepped up to be a single father to his son. Neither Joshua nor Dave hadn't heard from Jane for over four years. Dave thought she now was living somewhere in Scotland on a farm. Joshua looked over at his dad and was glad he had been able to make his life more financially comfortable by making his vlogs. He just wished that the idea of this stunt hadn't been welcomed so much by his dad and Sarah Keen and that he had stood up to both of them and refused to take part.

The director Jami came over to Joshua. "Doing great my man," he said cheerfully. "Looks like you are getting the idea. We'd like to do a run through now before the weather gets worse. Don't worry if you fluff it, we'll keep the cameras running so you can carry on."The crew positioned the experts on the edge of the ledge, with Joshua behind them.

"And action!" yells Jami.

One by one each of the parkour crew leap across, one managing to jump up the wall before making the leap across at an impossible angle. Then it was Joshua's turn. He gulped and ran for it. As he reached the edge his foot caught on one side of the ledge and instead of leaping across his momentum took him downwards instead. A strong gust of wind at the wrong moment made him twist in mid air coming more head first than feet first, and as he crashed to the ground, he missed some pedestrians by inches.

They leapt back horrified before looking up to see where he had come from. Above the pedestrians, the parkour crew looked down from the ledge they had all reached, and Sarah and Dave looked down on him sprawled out in a widening pool of blood face up looking startled. Joshua's heart flutters briefly then it starts again. His breathing stops, but he doesn't die.

* * *

999 calls came in thick and fast, both from the pedestrians and also the filming crew, plus a frantic Dave and Sarah Keen. Police and Ambulance teams respond as they arrive two of the pedestrians were checking Joshua for vital signs but sensibly they do not try and move him as they can see he has a pulse. One is attempting resuscitation breaths carefully as the paramedics arrive in a blaze of lights and noise.

The senior paramedic Carol assesses the casualty carefully, "Does anyone know what happened?"

One witness points upwards. "He came from up there, man."

Carol looks up and sees a group of people on the roof disappear.

..*Probably not a jumper then?*...

she thinks as she assesses Joshua's condition.

"Not breathing, love," said the pedestrian "But he has a strong heartbeat. I'm a St Johns volunteer, was a former ambulance driver in the '80s. Name's Kevin."

Carol smiles, "Thanks for not moving him Kevin, can you please go over to the patrol car there and give your statement?"

Kevin moves across to where the PC is talking to the other pedestrians. The ground floor door to the car park flies open and two people closely followed by a few more come racing out

"My boy," wails Dave. "Is he OK?"

Carol looks over at them "What happened, Sir?" she asks as she attaches an oxygen mask to Josh's face carefully without disturbing his head.

"We were filming a stunt," says Sarah Keen taking over. "This is Joshua Cooper, he was filming a parkour video for his fans. Please, is he going to be OK?"

Carol looks over at them. "He's critically injured. We need to get him to the hospital for assessment. Can you please follow us as I'm sure the surgical team will need to speak to you both?"

She looked over at Dave. "Does he have any allergies?"

"Only tomatoes," Dave said weakly "can't eat them, make his mouth swell up."

Carol nodded. "So no allergies to penicillin, other meds?"

Dave shakes his head.

The other paramedic brings over the scoop and stretcher, plus a neck brace and Carol stands to assist in getting Joshua's neck supported, then using the available pedestrians still around, she marshals them to get Joshua onto the scoop then onto the stretcher.

She calls over to Kevin the first aider "Kevin, could you assist us with holding his head in the ambulance please" Kevin comes over and agrees. Carol gets Kevin to hold Joshua's head steady as they manoeuvred the stretcher into the ambulance. The junior paramedic moves to the front of the ambulance and as Carol closes the door and sits down to assess Joshua more fully, she sees the PC come over to talk to the other people present. Blues and twos wail as the ambulance moves off at speed.

As the ambulance sets off Dave and Sarah turn to speak to the officer behind them.

"What's been happening here?" asked PC Jack Knotsford who had arrived on the scene at the same time as his colleague SPC Emma Bates. Emma took Sarah Keen to one side to ask her separately, as Dave explained what had happened to Joshua.

"I..it was an accident," Dave sobbed "He was taking part in a video for his channel..." He stopped talking, overwhelmed with grief. "Can I go, I have to follow him to the hospital?" Dave and Sarah gave their details to PC Knotsford then they hurried back into the car park to follow the ambulance to the hospital.

As they walked away PC Knotsford heard Sarah say, "I'll drive Dave, you are no fit state"

SPC Bates was about to start taking statements from the film crew and the parkour jumpers who looked very uncomfortable with the situation so PC Knotsford decided to start with them too. The witnesses to the fall had already given their details and left as SPC Bates walked over to check the place that the victim had landed.

She walked back over to PC Knotsford. "Looks like it was a stunt gone wrong", she commented indicating back towards where there was a pool of blood on the ground. "Not sure the poor soul is going to make it."

PC Knotsford nodded "Glad it wasn't another stabbing." They walked back to the group.

..This was going to take a long time to sort out...

PC Knotsford radioed back to base to confirm one injury was taken to hospital and it didn't appear to be a malicious incident. As they both began to take statements a pompous looking man in a grey suit hurried up to the group.

"Is someone here in charge? I was told that there was an accident on council property?"

PC Knotsford pointed out the patch of drying blood on the pavement "Not quite sir, on the path over there, but he came from up there" PC Knotsford pointed up to the roof of the car park.

"Better get health and safety out. It's going to be a long job."

He turned back to SPC Bates and winked at her. "Let him get the cleaning crews out on that one."

"Right sir." He turned to the leader of the parkour crew "What can you tell me about what happened?"

* * *

Later in the canteen, SPC Bates caught up with her colleague and pulled him over to one side of the room

"Got some news on that fallen lad" she hissed.

"We don't do that Emma" he hissed back. "Never look back over a call. It breaks your heart" as he pulled away she pulled even tighter on his arm

"No, she insisted. "I've got a mate at the hospital. She's just called me. That lad that fell off the car park, and the lad from the corner shop?"

"Yeah what about them?" replied Jake questioningly.

"They're both being moved."

"Moved where?"

"That's the point, my friend is in intensive care and she has told me the cases are linked."

"Linked by what? The lad was stabbed and this one fell off a car park."

"Their breathing, or not" she hissed back as several detectives walked past them laughing at a joke one had just been telling. "Neither of them were breathing right?"

"Yes, not surprisingly." agreed Jake.

"Yes but what is surprising is that neither of them is yet breathing."

"Again not surprising" commented Jake "They'd have been on oxygen from the scene."

"That's the point - they haven't been, and they aren't breathing, and they are not dead," exclaimed Emma frantically. "Paramedics got them to hospital and when they took the oxygen off to check their vitals their hearts were beating strongly but they weren't breathing, but they weren't dead, no matter how long they stayed off the oxygen. Something weird is going on and it's freaking out the staff including my friend," she hissed at Jake as more people walked by. "The two cases have now been moved."

"Moved where?" questioned Jake

"That's the point, my friend doesn't know. The families of the two boys were taken off by someone from Environmental Health who escorted them away, and the next shift my friend is on, both boys transferred according to their records. But it doesn't say where to, and that is not right. It always says where they have gone but not this time. All of the staff were just pulled into a meeting and told that the boys had been moved for contamination, but there was nothing on them. They were both tested for COVID and other things on their arrival. Nothing infectious"

Jake looked at Emma he knew she was right. He'd dated a nurse from the same hospital last year and when a patient had died and ended up in the wrong part of the hospital the management had freaked out.

"So two patients moved and their records don't tally?"Nothing we can do then Emma." Jake pulled her away from the canteen. "Just need to get onto the next call, but first a sausage sandwich for me" he turned away, then back to her.

"Fancy joining me?" She smiled bleakly as she replied "Nah, don't fancy watching you masticate" Jake grinned at her and went back into the canteen for his supper. Emma was worried though. Her friend Madeline was freaking out on the phone earlier. Emma had promised to go round to her house later with a bottle of wine.

Maybe I could find out a bit more about this?

* * *

10

Brian

Exeter

Brian laid back on his pillow...his oxygen tube a familiar part of his life since he'd succumbed to COPD, the nurses were nice here in the Ocean View nursing home though the water was only visible according to his granddaughter Katie if she stood on the loo and angled her head out of the window. That had set Brian off on another coughing fit which had alarmed his daughter Catherine who'd then scolded Katie for upsetting her granddad. When Brian caught his breath back he pleaded with Catherine not to make a big deal of it

"I'm dying chickie" Brian wheezed at his daughter. "Let her be. She's right...the marketing men here never promised me a water view out of my bedroom."

Catherine pursed her lips tighter. "Well, you did choose this place... we would have had you, but no you wanted your final resting place to be here...with your family limited to two visits a week..."

Brian sighed. "We've gone over this, chickie...that's COVID for you...they're just being careful."

Katie looked at the clock on the bedside table "Mum, we're going to be late for my rehearsal ." Catherine looks at her watch and thinks in a panic.

Oh God, the traffic will be dreadful.

She kisses her dad goodbye, ushering Katie to kiss her granddad's cheek before they both hustle out the door to his room, almost knocking over Majori the cleaner as she enters the room.

"Sorry, sorry," said Catherine as she hurried down the corridor with Katie close behind her.

Majori enters the room. "Mr can I clean please?" Brian nods his agreement. The coughing fit had taken his breath away more than he thought...

Majori opens the window overlooking the sculpture gardens below.

"Fresh air will keep you going."

Brian coughed again. His lungs don't fill with air. He starts to go blue, his eyes roll in his head, his breathing ceases, his heart continues to beat, he doesn't die...

* * *

Mrs Bateman general manager of Ocean View was enjoying her first coffee of the morning when the alarm sounds. She sighs and gets up crossing to the office door. As she enters the corridor one of the nursing staff comes running down towards her. Margaret is her senior staff nurse and is normally unflappable but she has an aura of panic in her eyes.

"Who is it?" asks Mrs Bateman

"Brian Aykland," replies Margaret "but there's a problem."

"What's the issue?" snaps Mrs Bateman. "He's on the end of life care."

"Yes," replies Margaret "and he's unresponsive but he's not dead."

"So comatose?" Mrs Bateman asks.

"No you'd better come and see," replies Margaret as she ushers Mrs Bateman towards the back of the block.

* * *

Two hours later.

"Where is he? "screams Catherine as she runs into the Ocean View for the second time that day.

As she runs down the corridor she's met by Margaret and Mrs Bateman who are flanked by some other people.

"Where's my dad?" repeats Catherine frantic with fear.

"He's in his room, but there's a problem," says Mrs Bateman grimly

"What? What do you mean? Is he dead?"

As she comes level with the group she realizes that there are some others in her dad's room. And they are wearing full protective clothing.

"Does he have COVID? Oh God, not that please" moans Catherine as she tries to enter the room

"Could you please come with us?" A young lady with a clipboard says steering her away from her dad's room.

"NO!" bellows Catherine. "I want to see my dad NOW!"

"Okay, but we need to talk to you first" The woman isn't letting go of Catherine's arm, and she has two young men behind her. Catherine looks at her properly and realizes she doesn't know any of them. Margaret and Mrs Bateman are also being led off down the corridor by another two men and they look scared.

"What the fuck has happened to my dad?" she asks as she is being led away

"Please Ms Cooper, come with us and we can tell you." Catherine slumps slightly then nods her head.

"Okay" says the woman, "in here please" gesturing to the room opposite her dad's room.

Inside are two tables and several chairs, she sits in one chair and looks at the woman

"Ms Cooper my name is Angela. I'm an Environmental Health Officer for Devon County Council."

" What?" said Catherine. "Had Dad got food poisoning or something? He said the curry was a bit off last night." Catherine trails off.

"No", Angela said. "Not food poisoning, he had an attack a couple of hours ago and has been unresponsive since. To be frank we don't know what's going on."

A man enters the room, Catherine looks up and recognizes Dr Patel the local GP for the home. "Dr Patel what's going on?" pleads Catherine. "Is my dad OK?"

He sits down opposite her. "No, I'm sorry Catherine he's not."

She sobs "Dead?"

"No", says Dr Patel slowly, "no not dead."

Then Catherine's voice rises again. "What the hell is going on.?"

Dr Patel gulps then says."We can't explain it." He hurriedly continues

"At 10.54 am this morning your father's breathing stopped, but his heart is still beating. We have taken him to Exeter hospital for an MRI scan, this has confirmed that he is not brain dead."

"What happened?" said Catherine, "how can his heart be still beating if he is not breathing?"

Dr Patel looked more grave. "There have been multiple cases in the county so far. We have had incidents that have happened in the last week and in all cases, the patient should have died, including your father. He is being moved to a special unit at the Army Centre near Andover. "

"Why for God's sake?" moans Catherine. Dr Patel continued "No medical experts can explain what had happened to Brian or the others, they have been moved to give the experts the best chance of working out what is happening to them and why."

Angela moves over to them both "We have transport that can take you and your daughter to where your dad is being looked after. We suggest you might want to pack a few clothes and things for both of you. This is a very serious matter and we want you to be informed as things develop." Catherine sinks back into the chair and sobs. Dr Patel hands her a box of tissues.

* * *

Angela arranged for Catherine to get a taxi to take her to Katie's rehearsal at the school. On arrival, Katie's headmaster came out to meet her. He had been briefed by the council officer before her arrival. He escorted Catherine into the theatre hall where Catherine found Katie chatting to her friends as they waited for their turn. As Catherine came into the hall Katie blanched as she saw her mum had been crying.

"Mum!" she wailed as she came running across the hall almost knocking over one of her friends in the process. "Granddad?" she sobbed.

Catherine took hold of Katie's arm and followed the headmaster outside into the hallway. He gestured for them to go into a classroom where Catherine sat down on one of the chairs set out.

"Darling your Granddad is not well, but he is not dead" Catherine stated frankly. "Something had happened to him, and it's happened to others in the area. We are going home to pack and a taxi is coming to take us to where he is being looked after" Katie sobbed harder and Catherine hugged her daughter as she sobbed.

"What's happened to him?" Katie asked as she looked up at her mum, her face full of fear and worry.

Catherine replied "I don't really understand it love, but he is not dead" she added fiercely."Come on, let's collect your bag and we can talk on the way home." Catherine and Katie went back out into the corridor. Catherine briefly confirmed to the Headmaster that Katie wouldn't be at school for a few days. As they walked out into the sunshine Catherine felt weak with worry

...How is my dad alive if he isn't breathing...

Catherine and Katie got into the taxi which had brought Catherine to the school. It took them back to the Ocean View for Catherine to collect her car and drive home to pack. Three hours later Catherine and Katie were packed and waiting for the driver to take them to where Brian was fighting for his life. Katie had cried constantly on the journey home, but as she got into their house, Katie had started to help Catherine decide what they needed to do. Catherine looked over at her daughter as she sat in her favourite armchair making lists of things that they needed to do before they left. Catherine had always been proud of her daughter but she was beginning to realise just how grown up her Katie really was.

* * *

11

COBRA

Guy Wright, Special Science advisor finishes his briefing to the British Government cabinet and turns to the Prime Minister. "Any questions Sir?" he asks politely.

"Well yes," said Prime Minister Howard Taylor. "What you're saying is if a madman came here and shot me in the head I wouldn't die?"

"No, Sir. What we are saying is for all these cases." He indicates the map behind him.

"None of these people died when they should have done" he turns back to the Cabinet "and if this has spread beyond Devon and the South East, say to the whole of the country, well no Prime Minister you would live but we couldn't guarantee what your life would be like and infections would no longer see you off. It would be a living hell."

"So zombies then?" asks political advisor James Bedgrove.

"No," said Guy Wright " they've NEVER been dead...Can't be dead, but they SHOULD have died. All of them, injuries beyond what medical science suggests is liveable"

" NBD's," suggests Mark King the Chancellor looking pale and drawn. "Not been dead's."

Guy Wright moves across to a map of South Devon.

"Sir, it appears to have started in Devon."

Looking at the map Howard could see tracks of dots radiating out across the county...

"In these areas, we could expect to see over the course of the last few days over 250 deaths from various causes, from natural death due to ageing"

"COVID," pipes up another advisor, Jenny Green.

"Yes COVID," agrees Guy

"We have about three fatal cases a month in the South West at the moment, plus there are fatal RTA's Road Traffic accidents, fires, falls, and especially around the south coast a lot of elderly people succumbing to their illnesses ."

The map behind them shows a series of dots, green and red.

"The green dots Sir, are from normal deaths, the heart stops, brain death occurs, the patient is pronounced. The red dots are the ones we cannot explain. Eight deaths so far, one RTA where death should have occurred."

A soft cough behind him...standing straight behind him was Wing Commander Cooke who added

"Prime Minister, our best guess is that whatever happened it's started here." He pointed to the area to the south of Exeter. "And the first reports suggest some time after last Thursday."

"From our first reports accidents, RTA's, murders, suicides and other normally fatal incidents just aren't and we don't know why. People's breathing stops but their hearts keep beating and in two of the cases so far brain stem death is NOT confirmed, we do not have any idea why."

He moves around to face the Prime Minister.

"One case, Sir, is a particularly horrific one, one of the first we think. A young couple RTA near Exeter, car smashes into trees at high speed, suspecting the driver was high and carrying substantial quantities of alcohol which caught fire and exploded."

Howard pales and sits back down. "Dead?" He whispers as he runs his fingers through his hair.

"No," Wing Commander Cooke replies. "That's the problem. They are not breathing, the girl has lost most of her lower torso, her legs and one arm and both have horrific burns, but they are by some miracle still alive"

"No breathing, but their hearts are beating and they are not brain dead, though the lad should be with a massive chunk out his skull and burns covering 90% of his body, but he hasn't died. We can't explain it, and the Army Centre is also stumped. We've never seen anything like this ever."

Wing Commander then indicates the other red dots with his hand.

"Stabbing of a young lad in his family's shop, an elderly lady who had a heart attack, electrocution of a local builder, a head injury and an overdose. All should have been DOA, but none of them is, and the doctors and other professionals cannot understand how these people are not dead."

"So what do we do?" says the Prime Minister running his fingers through his mane of hair again.

Wing Commander Cooke replies, "All we can do for the moment is monitor the situation. We cannot predict who will die in a lot of cases. The people who are most predictable are the ones like the gentlemen in the hospice. He was due to die in the next six weeks, but so far, despite COPD, he has not died. His lungs have collapsed but his heart is still beating and every brain stem test we give him shows activity which means that death cannot be declared, so by the standards which have been set for the declaration of death for this man, "

Wing Commander Cooke sweeps his hand across the map. "And all of the rest of the people here and God only knows elsewhere, who are expected to die, don't actually die."

As Wing Commander Cooke looks out across the room, the severity of the crisis is reflected in the sombre features of the British Government cabinet members and advisors.

"Has any other country had a similar issue?" asks Health Minister Jonathan White.

" No, not that we are aware of" replied Wing Commander Cooke. "It seems to be a fairly localized series of unexplained events. We have taken the precaution of moving the patients to the Army Centre for security reasons. No hospital in the UK is secure enough, and the Army Centre has many facilities we can utilize. They have scientific and medical teams who are already welcoming the first set of patients to Hanger Three."

Wing Commander Cooke looked around the room. The cabinet committee all looked as sick as he was feeling. Howard Taylor looked over at him "Thank you for the briefing, Simon. We can only watch and wait to see what happens now."

* * *

12

Discoveries

After the initial meeting of the COBRA committee, Wing Commander Cooke had utilized the military medical teams to move the patients from the assessment unit at Exeter Hospital by road to Wiltshire. The journey was undertaken without fanfare but was accompanied by security rarely seen before. Local people living around the Centre were used to patrols and exercises, so they barely glanced up as the ambulances headed back to the Centre.

The road and perimeter signage proclaimed 'Army Medical Centre' but this part of southern England was about to become even more famous than during the infamous episode of poisoning in nearby Salisbury. The centre was located in a remote part of the county and had been used as an initial point for injured soldiers coming back from tours overseas. Since the withdrawal of troops from Afghanistan and other war torn areas, the centre had been underused until this crisis had developed.

The Centre consisted of five acres of secure hangers, and office space, with barracks towards the back of the site. Inside Hanger Three, which was situated in the centre of the site, a slick operation was in place.

Within a day sets of dividing walls had been assembled in the centre of the hanger. Rows of individual cubicles had been arranged with a hospital bed in each cubicle, and heart monitors and other equipment beeping reassuringly. Only eight of the beds were in use at the moment but Doctor Margaret Mitchell feared this was not going to be the final total she would see in this place. She moved down the row of patients checking the vital signs on the monitors by each bed. None of the patients was conscious, none responded to their care by dedicated nurses.

The eerie lack of respirator sounds made her shudder internally. It was the most difficult part of the whole situation for her and her colleagues. Once it had been established that none of the patients was breathing, but they were not dead, it seemed unnecessary for the staff to set up oxygen tanks for patients who did not appear to need them.

Several of the nurses who were deeply religious were given special leave to move to another area, as they found the situation unbearable. One nurse from East Timor shuddered and crossed herself when she was asked if she wanted to work in the unit. She declined and was moved to a unit looking after the well being of the staff on site.

In a separate part of the hanger were the two most distressing cases, shielded by curtains and another wall. A young man who had been so badly burned he was reduced to at most a torso, head and one leg. His arms and other leg had not been salvageable, though Dr Mitchell thought with grim contemplation, the young man should not be alive, none of the patients she was looking after should be alive.

The man's companion was on the other bed. A young girl who had only her head, her face burned so badly she could not be identified, one arm and her torso. The remaining parts of her legs and the other arm were still in the vehicle she had been in which crashed. The girl's heart and brain stem were all in perfect working order but she was not breathing. Both the man and woman had layers of special burns dressing across their heads and what remained of their bodies, though Dr Mitchell had been informed by the team leader for burns, that it was very unlikely that either of these two patients would survive for very much longer. The complications of third degree burns can and often include infections, blood loss and shock.

The best qualified scientific and medical teams had already established that there was no immediate reason as to why these people were left in this limbo. The tests were continuing round the clock and the best minds in these areas in the UK and around the world were searching for an answer and a solution to this grim situation.

Dr Mitchell walked down the corridor to the conference room and joined the team who were briefing the Government committee. Both on the screen and in the room no one spoke as Mari Gushand the senior scientist at The Army Centre gave an update. Professor Kingston the Chief Medical Officer looked ashen as did most of the others present including Prime Minister Howard Taylor. Mari Gushand gestured back to the screen on the wall behind her.

"This is a sample of cerebrospinal fluid which for those present in the room without a medical degree is a clear fluid that surrounds the brain and spinal cord. It cushions the brain and spinal cord from injury and also serves as a nutrient delivery and waste removal system for the brain. This fluid should be clear but as you can see there are particles present that should not be there."

She turns back to the room. "We have now tested samples from each and every one of the patients and each and everyone has the same anomaly present. Each person has the same particles present, but as of this morning, we do not know why these particles are inside the fluid or inside the patients. It defies any logical explanation"

Professor Kingston looked up and asked, "What are these particles? Bacteria, viruses, fungi?

Mari looked at each of them. "Our first indication is that these particles are dust, more specifically cosmic rock dust."

The room erupted as many voices asked questions at the same time. Mari put up her hand for quiet.

"Please, one at a time, ladies and gentlemen."

Prime Minister Howard Taylor asked the next question. "Is this only present in the patients? not the staff or those looking after them? Not infectious?"

Mari nodded to the Prime Minister and the room.

"Yes, Prime Minister there is no indications that anyone else who has come into contact with any of the patients has the same infection in their fluid, and to be sure we have requested lumbar punctures for anyone coming into contact with them. Nothing has shown up so far. Each case is unique yet for some reason is also linked and so far the only link we can find is the fact that each of these people should have died, so our suggestion is that somehow each of these people were infected by something and that has prevented their deaths."

"Is it alien," said one of the advisors who looked like he would throw up.

"Technically yes," said Mari, then continued quickly " in so much as most of what is on earth including us is from other worlds. We all originated as dust, and as a recent report on PBS mentioned over sixty tons of cosmic dust falls on the earth every day, then technically this dust is just more of the same."

Mari pauses. "We cannot explain why these people have not died as expected and so far the only link is here in their spinal fluid. We are working around the clock with colleagues in other countries to identify why this dust is in their bodies and what it is doing. Our colleagues in the US are pursuing some leads relating to the blood-brain barrier"

Another advisor put their hand up on the screen "Is there going to be testing of people in the same area these patients came from? Their friends and family?" Mari confirmed that limited testing of family and close contacts of the patients has already started but as lumbar punctures were a risky operation, this was unlikely to be as successful. The meeting was adjourned until the following morning.

Mari walked out of the room to find her colleague Sam Knott waiting for her.

"Mari, we have a call waiting from CDC." They walked down the corridor and into another meeting room where a screen showed a room full of officials in military uniform. Mari and Sam sat down and on screen the head of the meeting spoke.

"Ms Gushand, your reputation proceeds you over here. My name is General Adams, my colleagues here," he indicates the room "are all CDC employees. We have studied the samples that have been sent to us, and we agree that the contaminant is dust, and yet we cannot see any good reason why it should have penetrated the blood-brain barrier. We have seen this of course as have you in MS - Multiple sclerosis patients but the cells crossing over in those cases are attacking the myelin around the nerves. This substance appears to be in all cases protecting the brain and somehow the heart to prevent brain death as would normally be the case."

Mari commented, "Yes we agree somehow these particles appear to be assisting both the heart and the brain, which would normally result in brain death after a few minutes of the heart stopping. The most interesting case is that of the electrocuted man who appears to have started his own heart after receiving a massive shock. The paramedic on site couldn't explain the readings he was getting. I think you have received those as well?"

"Yes ma'am we have. I agree as does my team, that the heart rhythms of that patient are troubling."

Mari continued "The other cases are also as disturbing and also fascinating. We have a gentleman here with COPD, and secondary heart issues, whose latest results appear to show his heart is not only beating strongly, but without knowing that he was in poor health, we would have assumed his heart to be that of a much younger man. We have come to a preliminary conclusion that this dust is helping these people in some way and making them less vulnerable to other problems associated with their injuries or illnesses. The gentleman with COPD like the others isn't breathing, but that seems to not be causing his health any issues. We are however most concerned with the two burn patients. Both of them are in very poor health and yet the usual expectation of infections, shock and fluid loss at the moment does not appear to have occurred. The lady who had a massive heart attack has not succumbed to her injuries, nor have any of the others. We simply cannot understand what has happened to these people or why them, and not others.

General Adams nodded in agreement. "We can only keep looking for answers Ms Gushand, the UK, the US and the rest of the world."

Mari nodded, and after a short discussion about the next steps, the meeting was ended. Sam Knott and Mari then left the conference room for more testing to be started. Mari mused

...something is keeping these people alive, but what is this dust to do with it...

As she walked down to the laboratories the conversation with General Adams played in her head.

Sam commented as they walked. "One anomaly the team did find, was a high level of dopamine and serotonin in their blood."

Mari turned to Sam puzzled "pleasure hormones?"

Sam nodded. "Yes, we did the tests twice as we thought they might have been contaminated." As they walked Mari continued to muse over the problem.

...Something happened to them, and now they are responding or being pacified?...

* * *

13

Consequences

Within forty-eight hours of the patients arriving at Hanger Three, the hanger had been transformed further. The medical teams decided that each of the cases should now have their own large room sound proofed as much as possible to give privacy, and space for family and friends, who had started to arrive at the centre to be with their family members.

Each room was now equipped with several cot beds for family members to stay. There was plenty of room in the hanger, and it appeared that these eight cases were the only ones to be identified so far. Dr Mitchell looked down on the floor of Hanger Three from the galley walkway running around near the roof of the hanger.

Each room had a clear perspex ceiling, so she and her team could monitor from above. Her office was in one corner of this raised galley area. She could see her teams below, carefully monitoring and nursing each of their charges. Each patient had their own team of nurses, overseen by her and her team of specialists.

None of the relatives of any of the patients now in the hanger was aware of any of the circumstances other than their family members hadn't died when expected. All were aware that other people were also in the same position, but so far, none of the families had asked any more awkward questions that couldn't be answered at present.

Dr Mitchell was expecting this to change soon, especially if and when news coverage of the patients reaches the wider world. She could see each of the families had questions, but she was bound by the Official Secrecy Act from telling them what she knew so far.

...So little information really, she thought. Why these people?...

* * *

In Room Two lay Samir in a stark hospital bed. Mr Azmed and his cousin Tamir who had flown down from Manchester both stood and watched him. Mr Azmed whispered prayers under his breath and leant heavily on Tamir to translate when any doctors arrive, as his English was not good. Tamir speaks to the doctors and the support nursing team when they enter room two but none of them can give him an idea of what is going on. In all his medical training, and in theirs too Tamir thinks,

... *No one had ever seen anything like this before...*

Tamir leaves the room and walks down to the canteen they have been given access to. As he walked by Room One, he sees a white couple arguing with the doctor.

...*This room has two patients in it, the only one he thinks, linked in some way?.*

"Get my daughter out of this room, that bastard caused this - bleeding drug dealer, I did warn her Margaret" the man indicates to the other bed. The door closes on the conversation from the inside and Tamir carries on down to the coffee machines.

In Room Five lies Jed Long, who was the only patient without any family or friends present. The paramedics that had delivered him explained that the patient had been found in a squat about to be possessed by the court bailiffs and it was the bailiffs who had found him lying in a room within the miserable building.

No one had come forward to claim him as their own which was one of the saddest parts of this story. Dr Mitchell had asked the police to try and track down relatives or friends from the squat. No one should be alone like this. In the meantime, his primary nurse Laura had taken to looking in on Jed when she wasn't on duty. Dr Mitchell knew that Laura didn't have any family or friends of her own outside the facility so she could empathize with a patient who didn't appear to have any either.

In Room Six, Brian Noble lies unresponsive with Catherine his daughter and Katie his granddaughter each holding one of his hands. Both Catherine and Katie had completely broken down when they were first allowed to see him. Neither of them could comprehend that despite having no breathing, Brian wasn't dead. Catherine could see on the monitor that Brian had a very strong heartbeat and the doctor had confirmed that his brain was active, even if he was unresponsive. Katie had withdrawn into herself at first but was now keeping her mum's spirits up.

Maisie Stephens had turned up at the Army Centre near Andover with her children in tow, once she learned of Barry's accident from the authorities at Exeter Hospital. Unfortunately, the security guards didn't have Barry's name down on their list of patients but after checking they confirmed he was there. Once this issue had been resolved, she and her children were allowed into Barry's room, number Four, and had not left since. Despite their divorce last year Maisie had never stopped loving her man, and she alternated between weeping and trying to comfort her children

* * *

In the canteen area, Dave Cooper and Sarah Keen sat at a table not speaking. In front of them are two cups of coffee, and noting the lack of steam,

probably cold by now?

thinks Tamir. He walks over to the table

"Would you like another coffee?" Dave looks up startled.

Tamir offers his hand. "Tamir Azmed - my cousin Samir is in Room Two."

Dave shakes his hand but looks totally bemused. "Yes please," said Dave.

Tamir gets three coffees and takes them over to the table.

"There you go. Can I sit down?" Dave nods and Tamir takes the chair indicated.

"What happened to your cousin?" says Sarah looking drawn and tired.

"Stabbed," said Tamir. "He was watching my uncle's shop and some thug came in and tried to steal some booze." Dave and Sarah look horrified.

"How about your family? Who's in the room - Seven isn't it, opposite to us?"

"My boy Joshua, he fell off a car park roof doing a stunt. Fell on his head," Dave says dully like he can't quite comprehend what's happening.

"Not dead?" asks Tamir

"No, just lying in bed, no breathing, heart rate is great, but according to the doctors, no one knows what's happened and why," replies Dave. "Have they told you anything about this?"

"No," said Tamir. "I'm a heart surgeon and I have never seen anything like this before, no pause in dying like they are experiencing. My cousin was stabbed in the liver, and help only arrived after my uncle came back to the shop early. Samir should have died, he lost nearly 90% of his blood, he shouldn't be alive."

"Neither should Josh," Dave replies. "I knew he didn't want to do the bloody stunt - it's all your fault!" He stands and yells and points at Sarah. "You persuaded him, and me, it was a great idea, publicity for the channel, and now he's..." he trails off knowing the words he would have used were "dead." Sarah shrinks away from Dave's accusing finger and sobs. She stands and staggers towards the ladies toilet just off the corridor.

* * *

In her office, Doctor Margaret Mitchell was in conference with the COBRA Committee updating them on the current situation. "What are we doing for them? The short answer is whatever we can. We've worked out that we can stop all infections, by making sure that their fluid bags have sufficient antibiotics. Our nursing teams demanded that we support the patients in this way including nutritional supplements, otherwise, these people would starve, but just not die. We believe that some members of staff have been in touch with the most militant nursing union, who are prepared to accuse us of war crimes if we do not support these patients to whatever end is coming for them all. The last thing we need Prime Minister is film footage or photos of British citizens reduced to skeletons who are still alive."

At the phone conference, Margaret heard the general agreement of the Committee. The Prime Minister thanked Dr Mitchell and hung up the call. Margaret breathed out a sigh of relief. She hated talking to people and her nerves since this happened have become more highly strung. She sought refuge in her work, and yet this work was probably the most nerve shredding of her long career.

* * *

In Room Three Marilyn's nephew, Jacob held his aunt's hand and talked softly to her. Beside him were three of the friends who had helped his aunt move to the sheltered accommodation, Baz, Jimmy, and Aiden. All of them looked like most of the other relatives, shell shocked and wondering if this was all a big film set. None of them had experienced anything like this before, and all of them thought of Marilyn as another parent. Since she had moved into Munstead Gardens, she had made it clear that all of Joshua's friends were welcome to visit, and all of them had.

Baz in particular was very fond of Marilyn who he had begun to think of as a second mum. Baz had struggled with university life, coming from a small town near Belfast, and yet when he had sat down on one of Marilyn's overstuffed chairs with a cup of tea and many biscuits, he felt at peace. He sat with his head in his hands, hoping he could have one more cup of sweet tea with this lovely lady again.

Earlier a Catholic priest Father John had come into Room Three and asked if he could pray for the family member. Joshua had agreed. He wasn't going to prevent anything from helping his aunt, even praying had come to him earlier. Marilyn looked so small and frail in the bed.

It was unnerving for all of them to see her there, not breathing yet her heart now beating strongly and the rhythm on the monitor showing that she was still there. Her skin colour was a healthy pink, yet she was unresponsive, and the lack of breathing unnerved them all. The silence from her lungs, no sound. Even a breathing machine would be better than this. The doctors couldn't explain it, and that made the whole situation far worse. No one knew why these people were all in the same state.

Aiden told the others that there were seven rooms that looked like they were occupied. He'd gone outside for a cig earlier in the day and had met Sarah Keen who was also hunched over a fag. Aiden felt sorry for her after she explained that she felt it was her fault her client was in this mess.

Suddenly an alarm sounded down the corridor. Aiden, Baz, and Jacob all looked up startled. Aiden went to the door and opened it up, followed by Jacob and Baz. They looked out and saw that on the wall outside room two, a red fire type alarm appeared to be making the noise. As they all watched, other doors opened and other people came out to see what was making such a racket.

Further down the corridor at the nursing station, three staff and a guard ran down to room two and entered. Aiden and the others came closer, and as the door shut they could see an elderly Asian man struggling with one of the staff.

"What's going on?" asked Aiden.

"Disturbance", replied another security guard as he barred their way. Aiden and the others stepped back but didn't leave the corridor. As they watched, the elderly Asian man was manhandled out of the room and down the corridor back in the direction of the nursing station.

Behind him was a younger Asian man

"Uncle - why?" he said as he too, was escorted down the corridor. Mr Azmed and Tamir were escorted to a room in the next block and left alone with the security guard at the door. Mr Azmed looked ashen, but resolute in the circumstances. Tamir looked like he didn't know who this person in the room was. As they stared at each other Mr Azmed looked furious but didn't speak.

* * *

Twenty minutes later Doctor Mitchell entered the room alone. "Mr Azmed, my name is Doctor Margaret Mitchell, and I am in charge of the team looking after your son Samir. I apologize for not being able to speak to you earlier, and I can see that you are both in distress."

Mr Azmed didn't speak, he just stared at her. Tamir said

"My uncle is, I think, in shock over this whole thing. I'm sorry that we had to meet like this. My name is Tamir, and I am Samir's cousin. My uncle speaks good English but if you don't mind can I translate for you?"

"Of course" agrees Dr Mitchell. Tamir rapidly speaks Urdu to his uncle who doesn't reply.

"May I sit down?" asks Dr Mitchell. She sits down on one of the chairs opposite the two men.

"My surgical team tells me that your Uncle tried to remove the feeding tube and pads from his son. Can he tell me why?"

Tamir repeats the questions but Mr Azmed doesn't reply.

"Do you know why please, Tamir?"

Tamir sighs and says, "Yes I think so. My Uncle is very religious and in Islamic tradition, the deceased is to be buried within 24 hours."

"But your cousin isn't dead" states Dr Mitchell. "His heart is beating and he had a brain scan when he arrives confirming his brain stem is not dead"

"No, that is true, but he is not breathing" states Tamir "My uncle thinks you are disrespecting his son, by keeping him alive on these machines, and feeding him when he died back in the shop. He wants him to die so he can bury his son." Tamir states flatly.

"And I agree I'm afraid Dr, my cousin died and now we want to take him to be buried."

Dr Mitchell replied. "If we took the monitors off your cousin, and removed the feeding line, he would not die, I am sure of that. He would starve in the most appalling way, but he would not die. That is the most horrendous way I could fail your cousin and the others in the same position, and I am not going to do that. I appreciate and respect your and your Uncle's beliefs but in medical terms, as you are aware, your cousin has not died. Therefore he cannot be buried, and will be looked after until he either recovers or he dies."

As Dr Mitchell looked over at Mr Azmed, she realized he did understand her.

She turned to him and said "Mr Azmed, my deepest and most heartfelt sympathies are with you and your family, but I am sworn to first do no harm to any of my patients including your son, and I will not allow him to suffer. If you are prepared to trust me, I will do everything in my power to make sure your son is not in pain, and not suffering. I do not know how this has happened, nor how to make it stop. All I can say is the UK and the world are trying to find an answer to what has happened to them." Mr Azmed nodded.

Tamir asked, "Is my uncle to be arrested?"

"No, not at the moment, but we will need to make sure one of our staff is in the room with you both from now on. I'm sorry but the care and well-being of Samir is more important," stated Dr Mitchell firmly. As she left, she realized her fingers were crossed when she stated to the Azmed family she didn't know how it had happened, though she also realized that she didn't know why, not yet anyway.

* * *

News of the attempted attack in room two spread throughout the other rooms and the hanger. Those family members not in shock congregated in the canteen a few minutes later to wait for news. Present were Dave Cooper, Sarah Keen, and Barry's ex wife Maisie, plus Jacob, Baz, and his other friends. They all sat looking around at each other.

Dave said to the room "That guy was here earlier - the cousin"

Sarah stood up. "Perhaps we should all introduce ourselves and our patients?"

No one spoke, then Jacob rose and said

"I'm Jacob, these are my friends Baz, Jimmy, and Aiden. My aunt Marilyn is in this place. I was told she had a heart attack, but it's not..."He trailed off and sat back down again.

Dave said "My boy Joshua is here, he was doing a stunt, and fell off a building"

Maisie said "My h-husband, ex- husband is here. He's a sparkie, e—e-electrician, and he had a shock."

Sarah took out a note pad and started writing these things down. "OK, so all of the people you are here for should in all cases have died but they haven't.?

All nodded their heads. "So what is going on? Sarah continued. "Why them, and taking the average number of people in the country, why all local? Is that correct? - all of you and the people you are here for are local to Devon?"

"Local yes all of us, I think" confirms Dave - "the Asian lad who got stabbed worked in the Seven to Eleven in Wood Water Lane, I recognized his dad when I saw them taking him off, used to get my newspaper there when I worked over at the factory down the road."

"My aunt lives in... lived in Paris Street," confirmed Jacob.

"Barry was working on that posh development down near the M5 Exeter Mansions, the yuppy one," confirmed Maisie

"So assuming the other beds are also being taken up by locals. What's happened in Exeter to cause this, whatever it is?" concludes Sarah.

"And why them?" adds Jacob.

Suddenly Baz looked at his phone which had just started beeping. As he did he looked up and over at the group.

"Something's up," he said. "Look at the news channel." He rotated his expensive mobile phone so they could all see the headline running across the bottom of the screen "

* * *

14

Breaking news

The pub in South Street Exeter was housed in an 18th Century former chapel. Like many pubs of its type, the clientele was mostly the students from the nearby university who would spend their afternoons in debates both great - meaning of life, and small - who's paying for the next round?.

So it wasn't a surprise that when the Satellite News Channel News banner appeared on the TV's mounted on the walls, no one paid much attention to it. That was until one of the students noticed the words appearing at the bottom of the screen. He rushed over to the bar, despite being earlier told not to,

"COVID regs" huffed the bar man, but agreed to turn the volume up and the subtitles on.

As he got back to his table he urged his fellow drinkers to stop their debate and watch the TV.

"Something's happened," he urged.

"Not bloody COVID again" piped back another one.

"We've had a year and half of those."

"NO" he urged "LOOK" - pointing again to the TV set which now showed a very serious news presenter looking back at them.

"We bring you breaking news from Devon" he announced. "We have reports of fatal injuries not leading to death" As they continued to watch the screen was filled with a shot of the outside of the convenience shop in Wood Water Lane in Exeter.

"I know that shop" yells one of their drinking buddies. "It's just down from my digs"

"QUIET" he yells, "I'm watching this" the table quietens down as the local reporter starts to speak

"We are outside the shop of Mr Ali Azmed, which has been the centre point for a story we cannot quite believe ourselves" She points to the shop.

"On Saturday afternoon as we reported at the time, a young man, the owner's son, was fatally stabbed in the liver whilst minding the shop."

She turns again to the camera "We have just learned that despite his injuries which were said to be fatal, the son Samir Azmed, is being treated at Exeter Hospital in a special sealed off ward."

"We have asked Devon Police, and also Exeter Hospital for a statement or comments, but have received none at this time."

In the pub, the room has gone deathly quiet. The barman looks around. Only when Boris announced the Stay at Home order in March 2020 has the pub been that quiet before.

The news report turns back to the presenter again.

"As we have more information we will bring it to you on this breaking news story. To summarize, a fatal stabbing in Devon appears to have caused some sort of complications."

As the story ended, one of the wags on the table announced

"See, told you - the Zombie apocalypse is here" and put his pint glass down.

"Better get another round in quick then," said another.

* * *

Sitting in her living room with a glass of wine Emma Bates nearly choked as she watched the TV. Her flatmate was out for the night, so she messaged Jake although he had told her he was going for a pint with his mates after work. A few minutes later he called her back.

"You watching this?" he said

"Yep, where are you?"

"In the pub, someone put the news channel on and the pub has gone deathly quiet. Not seen the pub so quiet since before the first lockdown order. Looks like you were right Emma. Something weird happened to those boys and some other people by the look of it."

Emma heard someone calling Jake's name on the other end of the phone "Never mind, I'll see you on the shift in the morning," she said. As the news footage continued she called her friend Madeline back to discuss what had been said. Their call went long into the night.

* * *

15

Broadcast to the world

The Cabinet room went quiet. They too had seen the breaking news story.

"Didn't we put a stop on this story?" said one of the advisors

Prime Minister Howard Taylor looks up. "No" he sighs again "We didn't want to draw attention to the issue. Seems I have got to get a press conference out tonight then?"

The Prime Minister looks at his Chief Medical Officer questioningly. Professor Kingston nods

The news reports quickly escalate from the first breaking news on Satellite News Channel earlier. Social media starts a massive storm with the tagline #deadnotdead heading rumours and hearsay from the local area.

* * *

At 9 pm the news networks break their usual schedule to the Number 10 Briefing room, freshly painted since the last COVID briefing. Standing at the centre pedestal is Prime Minster Howard Taylor and to his right is Professor Kingston his Chief Medical Officer.

The Prime Minister clears his throat and begins. "Thank you all for coming along to this briefing, which is also being broadcast live across the world"

The reporters present in the room look startled at this, no other countries have journalists present, only representatives, from Satellite News Channel, BBC, and the UK national press.

"What I am about to tell you is something I never thought I would be saying out loud. Please allow myself and Professor Kingston to explain then we will have time for a few questions"

He pauses, looks over at Professor Kingston who nods, and then continues

"We have received multiple reports from the South West of England specifically in and around the Exeter area, of cases of presumed fatalities, which frankly haven't been."

He pauses again. "In several cases, where medical knowledge would expect death to be confirmed, the patients are not clinically dead. Their breathing has stopped in all cases, but their hearts are beating strongly, and their brain stems are showing signs of normal activity."

Howard Taylor then turns again to Professor Kingston. "Could you please expand on this news?"

Professor Kingston looks over at the cameras.

"Firstly although we cannot yet explain what is happening, this situation appears to be limited to a local area in and around Exeter. None of the casualties have any sign of disease other than that which should have ended their lives such as COPD, injury, burns, etc .... but in these local cases, none of the deaths expected have happened."

He looks over at the Prime Minister and continues.

"We do not know why in these cases the normal process of death has not happened, and until we do, we have moved all of these cases to the Army Centre near Andover for further care and investigation."

The room explodes with noise at this point. The Professor puts up his hand for quiet "Please let me finish." The room quietens down but several journalists are on their feet waiting for their chance to ask a question. Professor Kingston continues.

"The UK Government have been in touch with the leaders of all other countries and as far as they are aware, nothing like this has happened elsewhere. We have received absolute support from our colleagues around the world, and they are all monitoring the situation in their own nations. We do not suspect a virus, as the cases are limited to a small area of Devon, and the presumed cause of these peoples deaths are varied and not linked in any other way other than that they are all in the same state of something we are having to refer to as 'not death'. That is a very crude phrase I accept, but in the face of not having any answers at this point, we are forced to call this something."

Professor Kingston continues, "However the tag line #deadnotdead isn't helpful either, nor is the social media frenzy which appears to have started"

The Prime Minister looks stern. Professor Kingston pauses and the Prime Minister looks over at the journalists who are all on their feet again

"Satellite News Channel," says a reporter rising from his chair looking rather pale and wan.

"Prime Minister can you please tell us when this started?" The Prime Minister looks over at Professor Kingston again.

"We believe that the first case happened a week ago." The reporter from ITV stood on her toes and waved at them both.

"Prime Minister, how many casualties have there been, what are their names, and what happened to them? "

The BBC reporter looks over and mutters to his colleague from the national press.

"Trust her to ask all the questions we all have." They both pay attention to the answer, Howard Taylor defers to Professor Kingston

"One for you, Jon," Professor Kingston addresses the question

"We cannot confirm the names of the patients due to confidentiality, as we are sure that hoards of journalists will be on their families' doorsteps within the hour. However, we can confirm as of this evening there have been eight cases in the Exeter area, and as I mentioned earlier, they have all been moved to a special unit at the Army Centre near Andover for further assessment and treatment."

Another reporter put up her hand, and Howard Taylor acknowledged her question

"Prime Minister, have there been other cases in this area and elsewhere which have not resulted in " she looks at her notebook "Not death?"

Howard Taylor looks surprised at this, but Professor Kingston and the medical advisors were expecting someone to catch on to the fact other people would have 'properly died' Howard Taylor looks at the reporter and the other journalists

"Yes I can confirm that other deaths have occurred in this and other areas with no sign of the symptoms that these cases have had"

The Satellite channel reporter lifts his hand again. "Prime Minister - the story Satellite News Channel news broke earlier this evening, that case is one of the ones you are referring to?"

Howard Taylor looks pale but nods his head. "Yes, that case was one of the first we have been notified about. Our thoughts are with the families affected in these cases, and we are doing everything we can for them and for their family members. We will keep the nation and the world updated as things develop" He then turns quickly and follows Professor Kingston out of the room to the sound of frustrated journalists calling their questions to them. As they walked back to the COBRA room Howard Taylor turns to his Chief Medical Officer and asked

"Do you think they will keep on digging, Jon?"

The Professor smiles grimly "Yes Howard, they will. This story is not going away anytime soon."

* * *

16

#notdead

The press descended on the location of the Army Medical Centre within the hour of the Prime Minister's broadcast. The security teams were ready for them and a cordon had already been established 500 yards from the main gate preventing access to the site. Security had been stepped up to unprecedented levels and guards with machine guns and dogs patrolled the perimeter and the grounds.

A no-fly zone was already in place, but this was heightened to include drones, and patrols scanned the sky looking for media helicopters or drones which were foolish to test the defences.

The site's Press Officer handed out press releases to the throng of media cameras and reporters and refused to answer any questions, directing these back to Number 10 when pressed. Despite the lack of information, a cavalcade of media broadcast vans filled the outlying lanes and broadcast from the centre.

One enterprising news channel realized that a local farmers' field was an ideal overlook position towards the Centre.

Unfortunately, when the farmer realized that media had descended on his field, he blocked off access and started his slurry sprayer systems from his tractor across the field where the news reporter was relaying to his studio team the view he had secured.

The reporter was in full flow, live from the scene when a gush of brown sticky slurry hit him from the right hand side, and propelled him further into the field. Next, to be hit was the cameraman, who quickly ran for the broadcast van to protect his equipment.

The van received the final load before the farmer hopped down off his tractor and headed home for a well earned cup of tea with his adoring wife. No charges were brought against him and the farmer became a local hero to those who had been disrupted by the media invasion.

* * *

Social media channels exploded with #notdead replacing #deadnotdead as the number one search across the world. The news conference headlined across the world, and every news channel in all languages headlined the situation with a variety of responses.

The president of the EU declared unity with the UK but plans emerged that all visitors from the UK would be refused on the basis that this #notdead situation could expand. These plans were shelved as it emerged that no further cases other than the eight poor souls had been discovered.

Joshua's channel soared higher up the ratings than Sarah Keen could ever have imagined when his fans discovered that he was one of the eight in hospital. One of the camera team shooting the parkour video had tweeted his "#notdead love and sympathy" to Joshua's family and this had helped the hashtag to spread.

It wasn't long before the remaining family and friends of the eight patients were doorstepped and asked for comments and or interviews. Mr Azmed's shop was besieged by tourists and gawkers who wanted to see the place where Samir had #notdied, but it was closed and the shutters were down.

The PC on door duty sent them all on their way. The shop had been fully analysed for evidence, including fingerprints on the box of vodka Samir had been protecting from Matty. A specialized cleaning crew had come and cleared up the remaining blood, but the chaos of the event would take a lot longer to disperse in the minds of the family and the locals.

Mr Azmed's wife stayed upstairs in the flat above the shop, with the phone off the hook. Her English wasn't great and when the phone had continued to ring, she just put the phone back down, then left it off the hook. It was quieter in the flat than outside. She sat on her son's bed and wept into her hands.

* * *

Through an appeal on Twitter by the bailiffs who had discovered Jed in the squat, Kitty was found and she was taken to the Centre to be with Jed. She had been staying with a friend after the visit by Mr C and hadn't heard about the eviction or what had happened to Jed. She sat bolt upright on the chair next to Jed's bed whispering to him to come back to her. Laura sat with them both, and Kitty found this a comfort knowing if she needed the loo, someone was with her man.

* * *

One indirect benefit of the Azmed case happened within a day of the first news reports. James Marston, Matty's accomplice turned himself into Exeter Police Station accompanied by his parents who had hired a top defence lawyer Jonathan Gribbs.

SPC Emma Bates & PC Jack Knotsford were in the station when the group arrived at the front desk asking to speak to a senior officer. Emma didn't recognize James Marston at first and it wasn't until DC Martin Smythe arrived to take them into an interview room that she began to realize that perhaps the case might be progressing.

During the next four hours, James Marston gave a detailed statement of what had occurred in the convenience shop and how James had not been aware that Matty had got a blade with him. James sat on the hard chair in the interview room and told the police everything.

He was horrified to learn that Samir had become one of the most famous people in the world at the moment - trending above even celebrities. He was more horrified to learn that he would be charged with aiding and abetting Matty in the attempted murder of Samir. The stark fact that so far Samir wasn't dead was a moot point in DC Smythe's mind.

His mother and father sat each holding one of his hands throughout the interview. The defence lawyer sat to one side making many notes on his legal pad. PC Jack Knotsford knew Jonathan Gribbs very well indeed.

Only five weeks ago whilst giving evidence in the court of a robbery gone wrong, Jonathan Gribbs had reduced PC Knotsford's evidence to shreds. In the end, the robber had got off on all charges, though the rest of the evidence was according to the Crown Prosecutor "mild to middling."

PC Knotsford wondered why Jonathan Gribbs had taken this case, as it was fairly obvious that James Marston was just an unfortunate side kick to the main star of the attempted murder - Matty Bartlett. PC Knotsford thought that perhaps being part of what was likely to be a unique criminal case would appeal to his ego.

DC Martin Smythe finished the interview with James Marston, and he was allowed out on bail with conditions not to contact Matty Bartlett or the victim's family. James left with his parents and the solicitor who shook James's father's hand before sending them off in a taxi.

DC Smythe then convened a meeting of the murder squad who were coordinating the hunt for the suspect. He confirmed the circumstances that James Marston had given including the likely location of Matty Bartlett.

Within two hours Matty Bartlett was in custody. He had been found hiding in his wardrobe at home when the police grab team had descended on Rushmore Towers, the rundown council estate on the edge of the city.

As they smashed in the door to his home, Matty had hidden in the large wardrobe in his room among the trainers and other items he had stolen over the years from shops in the local area.

* * *

The team read him his rights, handcuffed him, and bundled him into a patrol car to be interviewed. Another crime scene team assessed and photographed evidence including the knife used to stab Samir which was bundled up at the bottom of a putrid pile of clothing in Matty's room.

Matty's stepmother came back to the flat during this search and proceeded to rant at the officers who were "ruining her place" The PC on door duty smiled at her and suggested she might like to get a solicitor for her stepson. She turned on her heels, abused the neighbours who had come out to see the action, and returned to the pub she had come from.

On his arrival at the Police Station, Matty Bartlett ranted at the desk sergeant and was taken into a cell to "calm down." As the door banged shut, Matty realized that this was probably not going his way at all. He had seen the local news report on the satellite channel in the local pub and realized that his victim wasn't dead as he had thought. Not that Matty ever gave anything much thought these days. He just knew that swats like Samir needed to be taught a lesson.

The vodka he had stolen had been stashed in his room, and he had come home from the pub and drunk the lot. The resulting hangover meant he had spent the following day in bed, so had missed the gathering frenzy over Samir and the other victims.

Matty knew why he was in this place though. James 'grass' Marston. Matty had warned him on leaving the shop about what happens to grasses, and he was sure he had scared him into keeping his mouth shut. James had puked down the alleyway next to the shop and had run home to Mummy and Daddy in their yuppy home on the new estate bordering Rushmoor Towers.

Matty needed to get his story across and soon. He banged on the steel door of the cell until the weary desk sergeant came to see what the noise was all about.

"I want to make a statement," Matty said forcefully through the viewing flap in the door. "I've been fitted up."

The sergeant looked sceptical. "You've not been charged with anything yet, you are unfit to be interviewed so you can sleep off whatever you have taken. DC Smythe will be interviewing you in the morning, so you had better get some sleep".

He shut the flap and Matty kicked the door in frustration before sitting down again. His leg hurt, his head was still pounding and he knew he wasn't going to be able to talk his way out of this one.

* * *

DC Smythe woke Matty up early the next day, for his first interview about the attempted murder and robbery. Matty hadn't slept well in the cell. He had been woken often by the banging and clangs that happen in that environment, and he didn't have the benefit of being off his head either. He walked out of the cell bleary eyed into the corridor before being escorted upstairs for his interview.

Matty didn't have the benefit of expensive legal representation, unlike James Marston. The court appointed solicitor was young, male, and looked scared of being in the same room as Matty. The room had a large one way mirror and behind that stood the rest of the murder squad watching their boss grill the suspect. In the room, DC Smythe sat on the other side of the table staring at him smiling gently.

"Matty - I trust you are refreshed and able to understand the charges I am presenting to you? This interview is being audio and video recorded"

Matty grunted and didn't look up at him or his solicitor.

"OK, then I'll take that as a yes. We believe there is extremely good evidence to charge you with robbery and attempted murder of Samir Azmed. We have found the knife which we believe you stabbed him with, in an attempt to steal a bottle of cheap vodka from his father's shop.

It is being analysed at the moment, but we are informed by the lab that there are clear fingerprints on the knife, and we expect to match them in a short while with yours taken previously."

DC Smythe sat back satisfied.

"The booking in sergeant said that you mentioned last night that you had been "fitted up" Would you care to explain to us what you mean by that?"

"Fitted up by that posh kid. He stabbed that kid not me." muttered Matty as he tried to look innocent but failed.

"OK then, so you are saying that James Marston stabbed him not you?"

"Yeah, he wanted the booze so I helped him, but I didn't do it."

"OK, so you were just the accomplice. Well, we would at this point produce the CCTV evidence from the shop but unfortunately, we don't have any. Mr Azmed didn't bother with getting his camera fixed from the last robbery, and so we don't have that."

Matty looked up surprised, but DC Smythe then continued.

"However we do have this" he turned to the window and nodded. The door to the interview room opened and a mobile phone was handed over to DC Smythe. He turned back to Matty who looked puzzled.

DC Smythe then pressed a button on the phone to turn it on and turned it back to Matty who recognized his face on the screen. DC Smythe played play and a shaky video started up starring Matty Bartlett. On screen Matty was slurring and trying and failing to rap. It was obvious that he had been drinking and possibly taking drugs as he then proceeded to boast about 'skewering a paki'.

The video continued to run for another three minutes before it stopped on a view of Matty holding a knife.

"See that, Matty? The knife you are holding and waving about as you are trying and failing to rap in a constructed way? This phone and the video on it was sent to us anonymously by a concerned citizen, though we suspect it might have come from one of your crew who wanted nothing to do with you after realizing that you were likely to be charged with attempted murder. We believe that this is the knife you had in your home, stained with blood as you can see on the video. It's a remarkable confession really. We think the jury will be very interested in this evidence, and we think that you are going away for a very very long time."

Behind the mirror, the murder team smiled. DC Smythe always got his man or woman. Matty looked shaken and turned to his solicitor and raged

"You gonna let him fit me up?"

"Can I speak to my client in private, please?"

"Yes, no problem said a smiling DC Smythe - can I get you both a coffee?"

Both declined and as the door closed on Matty, DC Smythe smiled broadly as he realized that a small piece of justice was coming for the victim's family, though the complication of Samir being #notdead would ensure that this case would be making history for all the wrong reasons.

* * *

The political fall out of the #notdead patients continued to rage around the world. No further cases had been reported anywhere else, the initial media frenzy ensured that the cases would be top of the news. However as the weeks went by, and none of the patients succumbed to the injuries which had brought them to the Army Medical Centre, eventually, the reports started to fade out. Like other topical news stories in the world, the public got tired of the same information, and public announcements of the patients were few and limited in scope.

The UK government was forced to confirm, after the fourth week, that any patients who survived this crisis would not be detained, once it was established that they did not pose a hazard to the general public. The COBRA Committee was assured by the medical and scientific experts that it was highly likely that none would survive, and if they did, they would remain in the state they had arrived in. The medical and scientific experts were wrong.

* * *

#NOTDEAD

17

Revolution

Back in the canteen all of the family member's group look even paler than they were before the broadcasts on TV. They had all watched in silence, huddled around Baz and his mobile phone as the news presenter has explained what had been going on, from the public's perception, and an hour later watched the Prime Minister confirming the cases and their locality.

Maisie Stephens had left the group in tears during the Prime Minister's address to the nation and rejoined her children who were now in the nurse's canteen being distracted by one of the young female doctors who was getting thrashed at Karate Kick IV or some such game on their hand held console. Maisie had believed that Barry would wake up right until the Prime Minister's announcement, then she had lost all hope. She had never wanted to leave Barry but he was being such an idiot about her job, and she just wanted him to love her for all she had achieved, not just for the house keeping and children nurturing part of her. She walked into the canteen and noticed how tired her kids looked.

"Come on, you lot we need to get some rest so we can be bright and breezy for your Dad"

She ushered them back into room four, where they all kissed their dad and then lay down on the pull out stretcher beds at the other end of the large room. Maisie lay down but didn't sleep. All that she had heard on the TV was rolling around in her head and yet within five minutes, she too was asleep. In the bed at the other end of the room, Barry lay still and silent, the heart monitor flicked once, then started again slow and steadily. He did not breathe.

* * *

At the end of the news conference, the others sat back heavily on their chairs as the news coverage finished.

Sarah Keen looked up "Well they obviously know more than was said, that's for sure. Someone needs to tell us what the hell is going on."

As she finished Dr Mitchell walked into the canteen and addressed the group. "Could you all please come along with me?" They all got up and trooped after her like a gaggle of young medical students. She ushered them into a conference room adjacent to the canteen.

"Please, take a seat, all of you. I apologize for not getting together before now."

"No we had to find out on the news" fumed Dave. "My son is lying there, and you know what's happened to him, don't you? why he's lying there like that?"

Dr Mitchell paused to let him rant then said

"We do know that the cases are linked but we do not know why each of your family members has succumbed to this state when others did not."

She addressed each of them in turn

"Mr Cooper - your son was injured in Cathedral Quay car park, less than a mile away from another young man also received head injuries from riding an E scooter on the pavement without a helmet thirty minutes later. This young man died of his injuries. Your son is not yet dead."

She then turned to Jacob.

"Your aunt had a massive heart attack, less than two streets away, an elderly gentleman had a similar event in the middle of the local supermarket that afternoon. He died in the ambulance on the way to the hospital but your aunt is not yet dead. In each of the cases we have here, there have been similar fatal incidents in and around Exeter, Devon, and the rest of the UK, which have not resulted in the situations each of your family members are in." She paused briefly looking at each of them in turn.

"We are doing everything we can to find out what has happened and how we can help them. For now, we ask that you stay away from the news channels, as a lot of the information they are showing is assumptions. I am happy to talk to each of you individually or as a group whenever you need me to."

Dr Mitchell stood up and said, "I think you all need some sleep now."

The group remained sitting so Dr Mitchell left the room for them to talk.

"What do you think about that then?" asked Sarah Keen

"Load of cobblers," snarled Dave. "They know what's going on with them all."

"It's weird though isn't it?" said Jacob. "Why our relatives - when others did properly die. What makes them so special?"

Baz stood up and said, "I'm going to the car, I have an idea."

He left the room and came back a few minutes later with a road map and a pen

"Right, this is a street map of Exeter. I think we should plot where all of the patients were, and see if we can come up with something, a pattern maybe, that they haven't thought of?"

"Good idea," said Jacob.

They spread the map flat out on the conference room table and started to plot the locations. Each person mapped where their family member took ill, and when they were done, they had five dots on the map.

"The lad and girl in the car, where did they crash - does anyone know?"

"No, and I don't think the girl's family would be up for this. Don't think the lad has anyone with him either," said Tamir.

They all bent over the map and studied the area around the dots.

"Nothing's coming to mind," said Sarah "your cousin was stabbed here" pointing at the junction where Samir's family shop was,

"Your aunt took ill here," she addressed Jacob, who nodded.

"Jacob fell here," pointing at the car park near the Quay. "Does anyone know where the electrician was at the time?"

Jacob said, "Think he was working there." He pointed at a patch of green near the M5 motorway. "It's not farmland now, it's a massive housing estate," Sarah added a dot in the green space on the map. Catherine entered the conference room

"Hello," she said. "What's happening?"

The group introduced themselves and identified their family members' room numbers. Catherine peered at the map.

"You're plotting where they were? That's a good idea."

"Where did your family member fall ill?" asked Jacob

"Here," said Catherine pointing at the street where the Ocean View nursing home was situated close to the centre of the city.

"You missed the Doctor's little speech," said Dave. "She wanted us to know that they were stumped by this, but I think they know more than they are telling us."

"Did you see the news earlier?" asked Baz.

Catherine shook her head. "No, I've not heard or seen anything."

Baz passed her his mobile phone and she sat down on one of the chairs to watch the rolling news feed. Jacob looked at the map again. "OK we have five dots, the two in the car, we can only assume they were on a road somewhere. We have one dot missing"

"That's my man," said a small voice behind them. Kitty was standing in the doorway looking more fragile than ever.

"His name is Jed." She came closer into the room.

"He was here." She pointed at the street in the centre of the city where the squat was located.

Baz added a dot to the location she pointed out on the map. Baz smiled at Kitty.

"Hello, I'm Baz." He pointed at each of the others in the room in turn and introduced them all. Most smiled, except Catherine who was engrossed in the story unfolding on the small mobile phone in her hand.

Sarah walked over to Kitty and asked. "Hi, what's your name?"

"Kitty" replied Kitty in a small voice.

"Would you like a cup of coffee love?" asked Baz "You look like you could use some of the stuff in the canteen"

Kitty smiled at Baz "Yes please, milk and three sugars" Baz went out of the room and fetched Kitty a coffee. She accepted the hot mug and sipped it as they discussed the news footage and the information they had plotted on the map.

Once Catherine had finished with Baz's mobile phone Sarah coughed and tapped on the conference table

"Right everyone. We need to get a plan in place. I'm Joshua's manager Sarah and I have a lot of contacts in the media. I'm happy to be the spokesperson for the group if you would like me to?"

Everyone nodded their agreement

"Right. I'm going to need a list of your patients, what happened to them, and your contact details please."

She passed to Baz a notebook and pen. Baz passed on the notepad to Joshua who sat at the table and started to write down details of his aunt and his contact details.

Sarah moved over to talk to Tamir. "Hello," she said "Did I hear from the team looking after your cousin that you are a doctor?"

"Surgeon - heart surgeon" confirmed Tamir "but I have absolutely no idea what the hell is going on with any of the patients here, including my cousin" Sarah nodded in agreement. Tamir continued "but they do know something, I'm sure of that. The tests they arranged all seem to focus on their brains, but I can't work out why"

Sarah nodded again "Yes, Joshua had a lot of tests, though he did fall on his head."

"You happy with what they told us?" asked Tamir

"No, I know a whitewash when I hear it. They are telling us some of the truth but they have got a lot they haven't given over." Sarah watched as Catherine added her details to Sarah's notebook. "But having a group like this can't be a bad idea"

* * *

18

Awakenings

After constant, and heartfelt pleading from Cheri's father, to Dr Mitchell and the head of the burns team, she was eventually moved from room one into room eight. Dr Mitchell explained to them both that the centre only had limited qualified staff who could look after such badly burned patients. She also expressed her appreciation that in Cheri's parent's view, their daughter would not have been here but for the reckless actions of Ezake.

Cheri now lay in her new surroundings, with her parents by her bed. Cheri was brought up Catholic and her mother lay a cross on her bandaged chest, praying fervently that their daughter would be with her Lord soon. Neither of them wanted this to carry on, but their beliefs meant that, unlike Mr Azmed, they would not try to assist their daughter to die, that decision was for a higher power than them.

Father John had also been present with Cheri and her family. Fifteen hours after she was moved to room eight, Cheri finally succumbed to her injuries. She did not breathe again, and her heart stopped beating. The wails of her parents, and the alarm detailing her demise alerted the medical team to the sad fact of her passing. It had been decided at the beginning of this crisis that any patients who did die, would not be resuscitated. Father John spent some time with Cheri's parents who had accepted her fate, and he was instrumental in making sure that her body was released to her parents as quickly as possible.

* * *

Ezake survived for an additional five hours, but like Cheri, his heart stopped and he was finally dead. No one bar the medical staff were there to mourn his passing. An appeal for relatives or friends had gone out, but no one had come forward to be with him in his final hours. In both cases, death was finally pronounced after brain stem tests had been done. The postmortems had found no reason as to why either of these people had not died when they had crashed and been so badly burned. The only anomaly in both cases was that there was more of the dust found in their brain stems and within their lungs. No one could explain this and after more tests and samples taken, Cheri was given over to her parents for her funeral to take place. Ezake's body remained in the centre and was eventually buried in a local cemetery. No one came to mourn him.

* * *

Barry was the first to start breathing again. Maisie and the kids were eating in the canteen when Barry's condition changed. He had been receiving a bed bath from his care team at the time. As they washed and cleaned him, and began to turn him over, he coughed. Mike, who was the nurse coordinating the turn nearly dropped his head in surprise. As they turned him back onto his back again, Mike could see Barry's chest starting to rise and fall slowly. Mike pressed the alert button on the chest monitor and Dr Mitchell and her team came into the room to see what had happened.

Dr Mitchell carried out preliminary tests and was delighted to see that despite still being unconscious, Barry was indeed breathing again. Mike and his team completed Barry's bed bath and then went to tell Maisie and the kids the changing news. He found them all in the canteen eating sandwiches prepared by the unit's catering team. Hugo and Mark were devouring a bacon butty each with tomato sauce already in evidence on their t-shirts. Ryan aged twelve was eating what looked like a bowl of cereal, though he was mostly stirring the luminous coloured lumps in milk around the bowl. Maisie sat with a cup in front of her but wasn't drinking it. As Mike came into the room, he saw Maisie's face fall, he smiled at her broadly.

She stood up shakily and said fearfully, "Something's happened?"

He smiled at all of them. "Your dad's breathing again, kids." He turned back to Maisie who fell back into her chair with relief.

"Finish your breakfast. Dr Mitchell is with him at the moment. He's not awake but its looking better for him now." Maisie sat back down heavily and Mike could see the relief in her face.

Mike leaned over Ryan's shoulder and pretended to pluck a lump of cereal out of his bowl. "Better eat these up quick, Ryan, otherwise I might have one."

Ryan blocked Mike's attempt at snatching a cereal lump and started to eat. Maisie too, picked up her coffee cup and started to drink. Mike looked back at the family as he left the canteen. He hoped that his prediction was true for them. All of the families here at the unit had become very dear to all of the staff. He hoped that they would soon be able to go home with their family members. He returned to Barry's room to assist the medical team with their testing.

Barry regained consciousness thirty minutes after he started to breathe again. Dr Mitchell and her team had been monitoring his progress since the beginning and all in the room realized this was an incredibly unique moment in medical and social history. His colour had started to get better incrementally and when his eyes opened, he was shocked to see that he wasn't lying in a half built home, but in a clean, clinical room.

Dr Mitchell smiled at Barry "Good morning, Barry. My name is Dr Mitchell. You have been unconscious for some time. What do you remember last?"

Barry closed his eyes and said, "Water, in the bathroom, got shocked." His voice was fragile but clear to all.

"That's right Barry. You had an electric shock in the house you were in. You are in a special unit, Maisie and your kids are here" Barry opened his eyes wider and attempted to sit up, but started to cough.

"Lay back, it's OK. They are in the canteen." Barry lay back on the pillow and looked at Dr Mitchell, then up at the ceiling which was not the usual white polystyrene tiles, but clear perspex. He could see people above him on a walkway moving around.

"Where am I?" Dr Mitchell smiled at him.

"That Barry is a very good question." Mike pulled up a chair for Dr Mitchell and she sat down. Over the next twenty minutes, Dr Mitchell gave Barry a summarized version of the events that had happened to him. She briefly also touched on the other patients and the links between him and the others. She explained that he was one of six people in the world, who appeared to be linked by a unique marker. As she talked Barry closed his eyes. He was tired but her voice was soothing. After she had given him the first of many updates, Dr Mitchell patted his hand. In the doorway were Maisie and the kids. "I think you have a few visitors?" Turning to Maisie she said

"He's quite tired so don't be surprised if he falls asleep" Maisie came into the room with her kids all holding hands. Barry smiled at his wife who walked towards him buffeted by their three children.

"Hi, sweetie," he said. "Sorry to scare you, but I'm OK now." Hearing his voice, and seeing him awake and breathing again Maisie broke down and ran to hug her man. The kids too piled around him touching his face and weeping with relief. They all had never stopped loving their dad, they just felt that their mum needed them more.

Hugo felt the most relieved. Being the oldest child he was aware more than his little brothers of how close they had come to being fatherless. Mark and Ryan also understood how ill their dad had been, but they seemed more interested in how their dad was trending on social media now as one of the #notdead.

Hugo had tried to explain to them how this was just a phase and some other trending hashtag would come along and usurp their dad and the other people here. Even as he said it to them, he had realized that it was possible that that might not be the case.

Barry lay back on his pillow and smiled at his family. The medical teams couldn't explain what had happened to him, or the others in the same situation. Barry heard more about the others from Maisie who had refused to leave him since he had come here. His last memory before waking up to see her beautiful face was being in the half built home in Exeter and seeing a flash, then darkness.

That had been seven weeks ago, Maisie had told him. His kids had continued to weep when they had been allowed into his room to see him. He had wept too. He had nearly lost all of them, but Maisie had confirmed she and the kids were coming back home. They had sat around hugging him, and holding his hands which were dry and sore. The wound caused by the electrical shock on his leg had been bandaged.

He had been very lucky, he had been told, that the footwear he had on in the house had reduced the shock going through him. It was still a very nasty burn though, and Dr Mitchell had also told him there was likely to be pain, tingling, numbness, weakness or difficulty moving his leg. He was told how lucky he was that he had been discovered quickly. Barry didn't agree with that, but he knew that other factors had influenced his survival. He realized in order for him to leave and begin his new life, he needed to be compliant and agreeable.

Maisie had wept copiously when she had told him about the couple in the car who had not lived. She had been in the corridor when the medical teams had rushed to the girl's room with a trolley of medical kit, but later Maisie had been told by Mike, Barry's nurse that she had died. The young man who had been driving had died a few hours later. No one could explain how they had not been dead at the crash, but seeing the other patients all coming around, and breathing again had invigorated the staff looking after them.

* * *

The rest of the remaining patients in the hanger had become conscious over a period of forty hours after Barry had woken up. Marilyn had been the second to recover. Her breathing was shallow at first but got stronger. Aiden, Baz and Jacob had been in the room, and Baz had been awake and holding her hand. Baz had been leaning against the bed when he realized that Marilyn was breathing.

He had run over to when Aiden and Jacob were sleeping on the cots and shaken them awake. Jacob had run down the corridor to get the medical team to come and see, and after tests, Marilyn had opened her eyes to see her beloved nephew smiling with tears running down his cheeks. On the other side of the bed, Baz and Aiden hugged each other like they had scored a goal for England. Baz also wept freely. He had loved Marilyn like a mum, and to see her awake and breathing again was a joy.

Marilyn patted Jacob's hand softly and closed her eyes again, but her breathing continued slow and steady. Sometime later Marilyn heard from the doctor in charge Doctor Margaret Mitchell about what had happened to her, and that there were others in the same place. Marilyn didn't like being here, but she decided that if she was to go home, she needed to be compliant,

and I'm very good at that,

she thought with a faint smile.

* * *

Samir had awoken next in the dark. His last thought before he had fallen into the darkness was how angry his father would be to see blood on the floor and over the bottles of stock. Samir's breathing like the others was barely perceptible at first, no breathing machine monitored this function, so as each person had started to breathe unaided, it was the family and friends around them who noticed first. Samir's cousin Tamir was the first to realize his cousin's chest was rising and falling now. Samir's eyes remained closed for a while but on opening them, he saw his cousin mutter a prayer in Urdu.

"No need to pray for me, I'm OK."

Tamir pressed the call button next to the bed, and like the other patients, Samir was checked and tested, before he was returned to the room to be greeted by his father and cousin.

"Sammie, you are alive!" Mr Azmed stated, puzzled. "How is that possible?"

Samir shrugged, "Good genes Pops?" As Samir's breathing continued to improve, Tamir told him about the people also in the hospital, and the frenzy surrounding them all.

"You're famous Samir - all of you are," Tamir stated with a wide grin. "You and the other patients here, have been headlining around the world on all the news channels. Tell you what Samir, the local families will want you to marry their daughters now." Samir smiled but he knew that his destiny wasn't going to involve a three day wedding feast, and multiple kids. He had other plans now, just like the rest who had chosen. He laid his head back and smiled.

* * *

Jed was the next to awaken, with a huge cough. He sat bolt upright in bed like he expected Mr C to be standing there. He looked around confused. This wasn't the squat. It was a nice room though. As he looked around Kitty entered the room. She had been outside the hanger for another cig and had been talking to Laura, Jed's nurse about her man. Laura had been so kind to Kitty, and having been an intensive care nurse, she had reassured Kitty that talking to Jed had been good for him, and that sound was the last and the first thing to return to a patient. So Kitty had talked to Jed for hours and hours, but her voice was croaky now, so she had gone out for a break.

As Kitty entered the room, she realized that Jed was awake, and she ran across to him and hugged him fiercely weeping as she did so. Jed wrapped his arms around his love and smiled.

...Everything was OK, and Mr C would be delighted to see him again. I don't fear Mr C any longer. Mr C didn't know it but I'm about to make Mr C regret trying to get rid of me...

Jed smiled broadly as he hugged Kitty tightly.

...Things were going to change, and not in a way that Mr C could imagine...

* * *

Joshua awoke next. He also sprang up as he awoke with a massive cough. The noise woke up Dave from his fitful rest. The camp bed creaked as Dave tumbled off it, onto the floor. He stood up staring at Joshua, then came over to thump him on his back. "That's enough" wheezed Joshua," I'm fine."

"You're not fine," raged Dave. "You landed on your head boy, from thirty feet up."

As his voice rose higher, one of the medical orderlies came into the room and called back to the nursing station

"Got another one."

Dr Mitchell came into the room with her team.

"Hello Joshua, it's nice to meet you at last." She smiled.

Dave looked flushed but remained silent. Sarah Keen came into the room from the canteen.

"Joshua - you're awake! Great news."

She turned to Dave who looked mute. Sarah decided not to stay and went back to the canteen, where news of the recoveries was being relayed to the others. Joshua too, was taken to a separate room for assessment, before being returned to his room where his father was sitting.

"Glad to see you too, dad," Joshua said solemnly.

Dave looked over at his son, and couldn't explain the rising feeling of dread that had overtaken him on hearing Joshua's first cough. He smiled but inside felt fear.

...How had his son come back, from a massive fall off a really tall building and why was he now really frightened of his boy.

Dave wasn't a religious man but this seemed wrong to him. The whole thing felt wrong. He walked over to Joshua and patted his shoulder.

... Just wrong...

In Room six, Catherine was praying for a miracle for her dad too. All of the other patients were now awake and talking to both their families and the medical and security teams but so far Brian was not awake. Katie had reassured her mum that granddad would wake up too, but knowing the fate of the two burned in the car crash, Catherine wasn't sure about that. Catherine kept looking at her dad, so frail in the bed and wondered what his life would be like if he did wake up. The COPD was so advanced now, he couldn't breathe without an oxygen tube, and he struggled to do anything even with that.

Catherine wondered if her dad would be joining the other two in the mortuary. She also realized that with her dad not now struggling to breathe, his lungs weren't under such strain as before. Catherine looked over at the heart monitor which gave a reassuring rhythm.

Perhaps it would be OK after all?.

* * *

Katie came back into the room with a sandwich for her mum. She had grown up so fast during all of this, but she had realized that looking after people was something she might pursue in her studies. Until now, she had dreamed of a career in the media. Her school had a great media studies reputation, and she was also part of a theatre group. Now though all of that seemed so shallow. Katie had watched the nursing staff look after her granddad with such care and devotion. It had moved her to tears, and she realized that the path for her career wasn't going to be pretending to be a witch in some third rate theatre production, but instead was going to be a path to help others in nursing.

As Katie and Catherine ate their sandwiches, they chatted about funny moments and held Brian's hands. Catherine was glad that her daughter had been able to get to know her granddad before the COPD had forced him into the hospice.

Catherine was thrilled to learn from Katie about her plans for the future. Catherine had been supportive of her daughter's dreams. She had wondered what sort of a life Katie would have, and how long and how high she would be able to get in her chosen career of being an actress. Finding out in the last few days that Katie wanted to change her career to one in nursing, made Catherine feel very proud indeed.

Katie hadn't been aware that Brian's wife - Catherine's beloved Mama was a nurse in her early career before she gave it up to be a mother. Catherine found comfort in telling Katie about her nana Mary, who died before she was born.

...she would show Katie some pictures of her Nana when this whole horrible episode was over if it would ever be over...

As she thought that, she glanced over at her dad who was breathing. She clutched his hand and yelped at Katie, who dropped her sandwich in shock. Katie dashed out of the room calling for the nursing team to come and see her granddad. She dashed back in, followed by the lead nurse for Brian's care - Samuel Do Amaral.

Samuel was a deeply caring young man who had been talking to Katie about her plans for getting into Nursing. He had come over from East Timor thirty years ago and had worked as an Intensive Care nurse for nine years.

"Well now Mr Aykland, it's nice to finally meet you," Samuel said with a broad smile. "We're just going to take you out for some tests, then you can come back and we can get you a nice cup of tea."

Brian smiled weakly at Samuel and waved goodbye to his family as they wheeled him off further down the unit. Catherine and Katie hugged each other and waved back frantically, smiling and crying at the same time. They both felt like at last things were going to be OK.

* * *

In her office, Dr Mitchell was looking at the test results on all the patients that had started to breathe again. She was troubled by the whole situation but looking at all of these tests she could only wonder at what had truly happened to these people and why? She opened up each of the patient's folders scanning down the results of the batteries of tests done on each of them, from the first moment they arrived to a further series of tests done on them as they each started to recover.

...No recovery was not the right word for any of them. They were better than before. In all cases, the patient was somehow much less affected by the situations that had brought them here, situations which in each and every case should have killed them. All bar the burns patients. Why them? Why did they die when the others survived? ...

Dr Mitchell had started to come up with a theory.

...the wounds on the two in the car just were not repairable? All the others even the poor stabbed kid had terrible injuries or life threatening conditions, COPD, Heart failure, drug overdose, head injuries, and electrical shock. The markers for the pleasure hormones in each of them were incredibly worrying. They all seemed calm even when told of their similar symptoms which Dr Mitchell and the science teams had never seen. Fear anger, but not this eerie calm...

The strangest part of the whole situation was that none of the patients had so far expressed an interest to meet each other. Dr Mitchell had been part of the teams looking after other groups of survivors from disasters and crashes and in all cases, the survivors and the families of the dead gained enormous comfort from meeting each other. Not in this case, however. The link between them all should have been stronger than any other group, but in each and every instance of Dr Mitchell suggesting to the patients that they might benefit from chatting to the others, none of them had so far made any indication that this was wanted.

She wondered if the circumstances of each arrival might have been a factor.

...What would someone suffering from COPD have in common with an electrician who had been zapped in his workplace, or a young lad falling off a tall building. Yet each and every one of them had been linked by something she had no idea how to articulate...

All of the patient's families had developed a close bond shaped by their shared experiences. The meeting room in which Dr Mitchell had first met with the families, had started to become a family room for the whole of the group.

Dr Mitchell had seen Sarah Keen, the young gamers manager take control of the group, and Dr Mitchell was aware that she had been talking with a couple of media outlets. Dr Mitchell was aware of a couple of very limited press releases that Sarah had been behind, and these were just thanking the well wishers who had inundated Joshua's channel. Dr Mitchell had expected this to happen sooner or later but it added to her workload as it had been made clear for her to try and dissuade any of the families from speaking to the media.

She took off her glasses and rubbed her eyes. She had no explanation, and nor did anyone else. Some religious people would proclaim it a miracle, but she didn't see it like that.

...Somehow each of these people was "paused." That was the only way she could describe it. "Paused, then restarted - rebooted even." Dr Mitchell realized that this was the closest explanation - the dust had paused them, kept them alive until they could be restarted. Like computers requiring a restart when things go wrong...

She shuddered and stood up. She had meetings to attend now with the Government and the scientific committees. They would have their own agendas but having the power of social media behind the surviving victims would mean that the choices and options open to the government would be very limited. No restricted living, no confinement, no way of stopping these survivors from going back out into the world.

None of the tests done on them had shown any sign of infection which could have been a reason for caution, they hadn't infected anyone else, but she knew that somehow they were infected. Dr Mitchell knew this wasn't the end of this, she knew in her heart that this story had only just begun.

* * *

Barry stood at the washbasin in his room, lathered up his face with shaving foam, and with the help of his beloved Maisie, he managed a pretty good shave. His skin was still dry but he was alive. His kids and his wife were coming home... he had much to do now. Maisie kissed Barry's soapy face and left to join the kids for dinner in the canteen.

He added some toothpaste to the brush he had been given earlier with the shaving kit and brushed his teeth hard. He could taste the grit in his mouth ever since he had woken up. As he spat out the toothpaste, he saw in the sink mingled with the white foamy paste, small speckles of grey. He looked up at himself in the mirror and smiled broadly. The dust was finished in him, others would follow him, and soon all of them would be back out in the world to continue their journeys.

* * *

19

New start

Three weeks after his breathing started again, Barry moved back to his home in Exeter. Maisie and the kids were with him when the taxi delivered him back to banners and neighbours waving at him from their doorsteps. Hugo Mark and Ryan had shown him some of the footage on the internet including news reports on his and his fellow patient's condition. They had been delighted when their dad had come back, and Barry realized that they had no idea of how this would change all their lives. Barry like the others was briefed on the media frenzy surrounding them, but he like the others made it clear they wanted their lives back and the social media storm surrounding them, helped in their quest for getting out of the Centre as Dr Mitchell feared.

Barry had not spoken to any of the other patients yet. The rest were to be discharged soon, but he didn't need to speak to them to know what they were all thinking.

The voice reassured and calmed him. When he had first awoken he had thought he was going mad. He heard a distinctive voice neither male nor female but commanding and somehow reassuringly too

...It will be OK. All you have to do is get better...

Hearing the voice speak to him inside his brain was like a warm bath, calming and relaxing. He had heard other voices but these were quieter. The main voice told him

...you can hear the other people like you now but don't be scared...

The dust had given him that. They all now thought as one, a collective, and more would become part of the whole. Barry could be patient, they all could, they had all the time in the world.

The taxi he was in pulled up to the curb. Media vans were parked at the top of the street but a police cordon had prevented them from banging on their door. Barry smiled as he was helped out of the taxi into a wheelchair. His leg was still very sore, but it was healing well, but not too well, not enough to startle the medical teams, but definitely healing well. No need to cause panic, he felt great and his family were home again.

Shouts of "Over here Barry" greeted him from the end of the road. He waved at the media frenzy and neighbours as the taxi driver pushed him up to the front door. Maisie, Hugo, Mark and Ryan had run ahead of him to the front door and were standing outside weeping and smiling.

Above the door was a huge banner made of one of their bedsheets which had been roped to the upstairs windows and secured to the porchway roof- 'WELCOME HOME DAD' was written in large red letters - the boys had also added stick figure drawings of them all with 'Our Family' underneath.

As he got to them the taxi driver put the brakes on the wheelchair and helped him into the house, followed by the rest of the family. Barry had been given a pair of crutches to use around the house, and he had been warned to stay off his leg as much as possible. The driver handed over his medications, and the crutches and helped him stand to use them. The driver then waved goodbye and departed to more shouts from the end of the road. Maisie closed the door after him and said to the room

"Better get a brew on then?". All three boys leapt into action which made both Barry and Maisie chuckle. In the past, they had not been keen on helping but it seemed that these things they could all do, made them feel useful. Maisie helped Barry onto the sofa, and his crutches were propped up beside him against the wall. She still had tears in her eyes but she was also smiling broadly.

"Come here love," he said, and she sank down on the overstuffed sofa next to him. He took her into his arms and wasn't surprised to see she was weeping again.

"I'm home now love - all better."

She swiped his arm. "Not better - look at your leg, Barry."

The leg wound was covered in a special dressing to prevent infection.

"It's fine now," he said. "Be good as new before you know it. I'll be running around with the boys playing football by the summer." He hugged her again and thought

...or sooner...

He smiled again as all three strapping kids came into the living room with a huge tray of mugs and a packet of biscuits.

"Custard creams and stewed tea." Barry smiled. "I've missed those a lot, but I have missed you all more." Barry is then engulfed by his whole family piling onto him for a cuddle.

"Mind your dad's leg boys," Maisie warned

"It's all good," replies Barry who could not be seen for the bundle of his teenagers on top of him.

* * *

Samir had been the next to leave the centre. His father had left him in the care of his cousin in the last week to return to his mother and the shop. Samir didn't blame him, but he knew that it was unlikely that either of his parents would accept his return as a blessing. Samir knew that his father was uneasy in his presence and his mother had not come to see him in the Centre even when he woke up.

He felt their uneasiness clearly now, and he realized soon after waking that he could 'feel' the other patients, or at least the ones now awake again. This unsettled him for a brief moment until a thought popped into his head

...*It's OK, it will be fine...*

He didn't recognize the voice, but he knew it wasn't his internal voice. Yet he didn't feel unsettled anymore. He accepted the voice, he knew it was right. He was reassured and calm, it was going to be OK for all of them.

Tamir came into the room. He had suggested to his cousin that maybe it would be a good idea for him to come and stay in Manchester with him for a few days, and Samir had accepted it gratefully. Samir's wound in his side was healing nicely and Tamir could change a dressing quite well. Samir had smiled at his cousin as he was being instructed by his nurse how to do this task. She had ribbed Tamir gently about his skills but it wasn't meant to be mean. All of the staff at the centre had been uplifted by the return of the six, and they wanted to make sure that they all continued on their recoveries to full health.

Tamir helped his cousin into the wheelchair and wheeled him outside to his car. Tamir had refused the offer from Dr Mitchell of an escorted ambulance for his cousin and as he helped Samir into the passenger seat and helped him to put on his seat belt, he hoped that this was the right thing to do. Samir was paler than he had been. The effort in getting into the car had strained his wound but he smiled at Tamir and said -

"Come on then, cousin - I want one of these famous Manchester curries you keep on about, lead on!" Tamir closed the passenger door with a firm clunk. Tamir then went round to the driver's side, got in and tuned the radio to a popular Indian DAB station. The music pulsed as Tamir switched on the ignition, then set off to the north.

* * *

Jed was the next to leave the centre, the following day. Dr Mitchell had been especially worried about Jed and his long term prospects but neither her team nor her could find any reason to detain him any longer. He had survived a massive overdose and had been getting good hearty meals in the centre which had helped to fill out his scrawny frame. Kitty too had benefited from regular meals over the weeks and had developed a close friendship with Laura, Jed's head nurse. Kitty hadn't had any family for many years, which is why the people in the squat had become so important to her. Laura understood Kitty without having to ask her awkward questions, and Kitty accepted Laura's compassion without fighting it.

As Jed and Kitty's home had been repossessed, it took a few days to decide where they should now live. Eventually, after much pressure from Dr Mitchell, the local council found a small flat on the nicer side of Exeter for them to move into. Kitty was delighted that Laura lived only a few streets from the flat, and so was hoping that they would continue their friendship outside of the centre once Laura's secondment was over.

A social worker called Mr Tenson was assigned to them both and met them in one of the meeting rooms to explain their options. Neither Kitty nor Jed liked him much, but Jed understood clearly that he had to become

...complacent for a while...

He didn't really understand that phrase which popped into his head as he was thinking about kicking off in the meeting. Jed had never been one to accept authority ever. The authorities had put him in a hell hole aged eight and they had never looked after him ever since. He had to look out for himself, but things were different now. He calmed down, knowing that the voice inside him was right. Things had changed, but he needed not to become someone the authorities would be alerted to, not yet.

Mr Tenson arranged for the meagre possessions of Jed and Kitty's to be returned from the bailiffs and delivered to their new flat. Mr Tenson drove Jed and Kitty to their new home and when they arrived, Jed smiled broadly. He had only lived once in a place where the windows weren't bashed in and the roof didn't leak but he remembered that that place didn't go well. Mr C again, tainting memories of his time with Kitty. No longer he vowed silently.

Mr Tenson assured them both that their new home location was not known to a large number of people, as the council thought that when Jed's new home address was known, the neighbourhood would be overrun with media vans and pleas for interviews.

Mr Tenson parked the car outside the large house which had been divided up into flats on each floor. Jed and Kitty's new home was on the first floor with a view over the city. Mr Tenson helped Jed out of the passenger seat and Kitty from the back, and they followed him into the house. The house had a wide staircase leading up to the landing and their new front door. The door was a dark blue with 270B in bronze above a letterbox in bronze.

"There are three other flats in this house, the ground floor is 270A, above you is 270C and on the top floor is 270D. All the other tenants are also renting from the council, downstairs are a couple of doctors working at the main hospital" he pointed upwards

"Next floor is Mrs Hassan - she and her son Marcel are refugees from Syria - works at the council offices as a cleaner, and above them is Professor Andrews. He's a retired University lecturer - Maths I think." He took out a set of shiny keys and turned it in the lock. The door opened onto a spacious and airy hallway. Mr Tenson walked in, and Jed and Kitty followed him through into a small living room.

"We have taken the liberty of furnishing your flat with the basics Jed. It's all second-hand items but clean and usable." Kitty smiled as she looked at the large brown comfortable sofa in the corner. Mr Tenson walked them through the flat pointing out the fridge freezer, a basic but usable cooker installed in the kitchen, a large double bed with linen in the main bedroom. Large wooden blinds covered the windows but they were slanted to let in the sunlight from outside. He turned and handed Jed the keys

"This one is for the main front door, this one is for your door, this one is for the mailbox in the lobby downstairs, it's marked with your flat number." Mr Tenson looked at them both.

"You should be aware that any sign of drugs being in this flat or any unruly visitors to the building would mean immediate eviction" Jed smiled warmly at Mr Tenson

"Nothing like that, I've learned my lesson Mr Tenson" Mr Tenson looked unsettled at Jed's remark. He had seen many fall from their original intentions but this one did look sincere. Jed smiled even more broadly and thought

...*complacent*...

Kitty hugged him even tighter.

* * *

Dave Cooper sat in the centre's canteen with an untouched cup of coffee in front of him. He couldn't bring himself to be in the same room as his lad, his only child.

...*What was wrong with me?.*

He slumped back in the chair.

...Something wasn't right with Joshua...

Dr Mitchell had explained that head injuries caused behavioural issues with patients, but that wasn't it. Dave knew something else, something inside Joshua was different but he couldn't explain it. He had an aura of utter calm inside him, like an iceberg. He still smiled like Joshua, laughed at the cartoon channel on the TV in his room, ate for England still but it was like Joshua was a facsimile of himself, or a photocopy, that had been made over and over again.

...His essence wasn't there any more, but no one would understand...

Dr Mitchell had arranged for Dave to see a psychologist a few days ago. She hadn't understood what he was trying to say either. Dave was torn between voicing his fears that his son was "different" now, and possibly having him taken away, or keeping quiet, and then what? In the end, Dave just muttered about responsibility and how he felt when he saw Joshua on the ground, blood leaking from his head on the dirty litter strewn pavement. He could see that this is what the psychologist was looking for, so after weeping profusely and muttering about letting his boy down, she allowed him to leave. He didn't feel relieved, just fearful for the future.

Sarah Keen was ecstatic that her most valuable client wasn't lying in a morgue and she could see the opportunities for media interviews and promotional opportunities but Joshua had explained to her he was retiring from his gaming channel and so wouldn't be needing her any more.

...That didn't make any sense either. He loved his channel, video gaming and promotion of new games was his life before, now nothing?...

Dave had attempted to find out what was going on with Joshua, but he had just lain back against his pillow and said, "Dad, it's OK."

He refused to elaborate and so Dave was now sat here in the bright light of an empty canteen wondering how his life was going to change. Dave had agreed with Sarah Keen that it wasn't going to be a good idea for them to return home just yet.

Dave was worried for the future as well as his son. Joshua's channel has changed Dave's life as well as Joshua's. At first, when his son had made his channel, Dave had not understood the power of social media, but when Sarah Keen had explained that Joshua was earning over £100,000 a year simply by ads on the border of his channel and that was likely to be increased, Dave was shocked.

Over the last three years, Dave had not worked in his job as a factory manager and together with Sarah had managed his son's professional life. Hearing from Joshua he didn't want to do that any longer, Dave dreaded the call he might need to make to his area manager Peter to ask him for his old job back at the factory.

Despite being sacked by Joshua, Sarah had kindly offered them the use of her granny flat adjacent to her home for as long as they needed. She lived in a leafy suburb of Exeter and rarely had guests. Sarah had arranged for clothes and essentials for both Joshua and Dave to be delivered to the flat. Dave was grateful for her help, as he didn't want to deal with the media frenzy that had developed over the past few weeks and his home was still besieged by media vans and reporters.

Joshua's reluctance to engage with the media had escalated their efforts to contact them, and both Sarah and Dave had been forced to switch their mobile phones off to get some peace from the frantic calls and voice messages from newspapers, TV channels, and other outlets.

Three days later, on a bright sunny and cold day, Dave pushed his son in a wheelchair to a taxi parked outside Hanger Three. Joshua had spent time with each of the staff looking after him, thanking them for bringing him back. They had all been delighted by the polite young man who had hugged them in turn. As Dave helped Joshua into the back of the taxi, the sunlight glinted off Joshua's forehead which was bright with sweat.

"You OK, lad?" Dave asked worriedly.

"Yes Pops, just doing too much too soon. I'll be OK."

Joshua smiled at his dad and climbed into the back of the taxi. Dave went around the other side, and Sarah got into the front where she directed the driver to her home. The taxi had been arranged from Exeter so the driver was familiar with the address she gave him. As they left the site by a side entrance only one reporter, Simon Kendall was there to witness the departure. As the taxi sped by he noted down the taxi license plate and registration and got into his car to follow them.

Two hours after getting out of the centre, Joshua was being helped out of the taxi and into Sarah's home. Simon Kendall had lost them somewhere around Yeovil but he knew that the taxi firm was an Exeter one, and he would be able to find someone in the company to help him find Joshua and the story he knew was there somewhere. Dave, Sarah, and Joshua were unaware that their departure had been noticed.

Dave and Joshua allowed Sarah to show them her house, which until now neither of them had been to. All their previous meetings and dealings had happened at Dave's small terraced home on the north side of the city. Dave had always been protective of his son, whom he had brought up since the divorce, and now both of their lives had changed dramatically. She escorted them both to the granny annex to the side of her spacious home, which was bigger than the whole of Dave's house on the other side of the city. As they walked into the huge downstairs room which had been split into a living room and kitchen Dave smiled at Sarah and said

"Nice place, no Granny in it though?"

She smiled back thinly "My mother lived here until she went into a care home last year"

Dave blushed and Joshua sniggered. Sarah showed them around the annexe and gave Dave the keys.

"No pressure, stay as long as you like." She turned to Joshua. "Sometime next week can we go through your remaining contracts as we need to close them down? The advertisers have been delighted as your channel has gone from 501st to nearly in the top ten on the gaming charts."

Dave turned to Sarah - "How much money had Joshua made since the fall?"

Sarah smiled. "The accountants called me last week, it coming in at about £400,000."

Dave gulped visibly and sat down on one end of the sofa. "£400k in advertising revenue, in eight weeks!?" He turned to Joshua who was examining a colourful oil painting on one of the walls.

"Josh - did you hear that?!"

Joshua turned and smiled at them both.

"I heard you, but it doesn't make any difference. I'm quitting. I've got other plans." Dave exploded back onto his feet and dashed over to Joshua who had stepped back. "Joshua - you could be a millionaire by next year, doesn't that give you choices later on in life? carry on working on your channel and you can then retire and do what you want where you want"

Joshua smiled again. "Maybe" He turned back to the painting and said to Sarah "I really like that picture." Sarah smiled back at him. She had never known Joshua to be interested in art before.

"Glad you like it, it's by an artist called Jean Claude Tron. Its one of my favourites too - its called 'La Lumière de Provence'. It's what's known as a giclee, it's a special type of print. You could probably afford the original to this one Joshua, if not now then certainly by next year, but only if you go back to what you are really good at."

Joshua looked at her steadily. "No more Parkour?"

"No more stunts!" Sarah exclaimed passionately "Just you in your studio doing what you are really good at, and inspiring others with your passion for gaming."

Joshua looked at his dad. Inside his head, he heard a voice whispering the word

..Compliant...

He sort of knew what that word meant - fit in, don't be obvious. His mind calmed and he felt warm and safe. He smiled back at them both.

"OK, I'll give it a go. Not even sure I can actually still play though."

Sarah smiled at him "I've got the latest console up in my study - did you want to have a go at it and see if you can beat a couple of oldies?"

Joshua smiled broadly "Easy!."

Dave smiled back at his boy but inside he was still feeling this was all wrong. He couldn't explain it but something wasn't right with Joshua. It wasn't the head injury - he knew that those can make people differ in their personalities but something else, something intangible.

Sarah came back into the room with a large box. "Come on then Joshua, help me get this set up and you can thrash me at #fightclub or whatever you like."

Dave watched his son expertly set up the console behind Sarah's large HDTV in the living room and then as she predicted, thrashed both her and Dave at every level. Sarah pleaded for a break and beckoned Dave out into the garden.

"So what do you think, Dave?" Do you think he will come around?"

Dave shrugged. "Not sure he should be gaming for long hours each day; he's just come out of the hospital."

Sarah patted his shoulder. "Of course, no, I was thinking just intro sessions to start off with." She smiled at him. "It's going to be OK Dave, I promise." Dave wasn't sure that was a promise she could actually make. All he could do was watch and wait.

In the living room, Joshua was gaming better than he ever did before. He was also aware of his dad's reticence about him. The voice inside him whispered reassuringly to him. The Joshua sitting in the living room was also in some small part of him, the Joshua whom he had been before the dust. Without the dust, he knew that body would have died. Like the others, all of them were closer to death than any of them had realized. Joshua knew he needed to act the same as this body was before, and if that meant waiting for a while, he could do that. Sarah and Dave came back into the room

"Come on Dad, let me thrash you again?" Dave looked over at Joshua and began for a moment to see the child he had raised.

...*Maybe this was all down to the shock of the accident after all?.*

Dave smiled back "I'll thrash you!" as he came over and sat beside his boy." Joshua smiled back at him, and Sarah looked on as they played and joshed each other and giggled.

* * *

Back in the centre, Marilyn was leaving a meeting with Doctor Margaret Mitchell. Her nephew and his friends helped push her out of the meeting room in her wheelchair which they had nicknamed 'Doris.' Marilyn was grateful for their support but she was also very clear to them and Dr Mitchell that she wasn't prepared to stay in the centre for very much longer.

Marilyn knew like the rest of the survivors that her healing had become slower than it could be, but in order not to attract attention the dust had made sure that her heart function had not shown too much improvement after such a massive cardiac attack. All of the ECG tests that the medical teams had done on her, didn't appear to alert them to anything. She knew that this was also the case in the other patients, all of them were healing at the approximate pace which was expected. Jacob, Baz, Jimmy, and Aiden had all stayed with her throughout this ordeal, but it was time now for their lives to begin again.

"Jacob, can you please call Lisa and arrange for a taxi for me to go home?"

Jacob turned to his aunt sitting in her wheelchair. "Are you sure Auntie Marilyn?"

"Yes," Marilyn replies firmly. "Time for you boys to get back to your classes and make me even more proud than I already am" Baz blushed the hardest but all four of them looked suitably relieved.

Jacob and his friends had brought their laptops to the centre after a few days and were on zoom lectures for a lot of the day. The canteen was very busy with the staff, so Dr Mitchell had offered them all the use of one of the many meeting rooms in the centre.

Jacob and his mates had gratefully accepted and some sort of normality for these students had begun. All of them were used by now to remote lectures after the last sixteen months, but they all missed the social joshing and fun now coming back to the University.

"OK, but I am not going back to my digs, Auntie Marilyn, not for a while. I'm going to stay in the family flat at your sheltered housing for a few days." Marilyn nodded her agreement to this, it would be nice to see Jacob more often, but it was a bit inconvenient for her future plans. The dust would have to continue to assist her heart healing but not at the pace she knew it could be. Still, she had all the time she needed now, all of the patients did.

She smiled at all of them. "That sounds very nice indeed, but all of you are welcome for afternoon tea." Baz in response hugged his favourite elderly person and traded slaps with Aiden and Jimmy who also loved to spend time drinking tea and eating biscuits with Marilyn.

* * *

The following day, Marilyn and her nephew were driven back to Exeter by the same driver who had collected Barry. Aiden, Jimmy, and Baz followed in Baz's wreck of a car - a very old and rusty Ford Ka, held together as the others frequently told Baz, "by the rust and the will of God, but mostly rust."

The taxi driver who had been arranged to collect Marilyn was called Arthur Cook, and he was hoping to make a very large amount of money. Simon Kendall the journalist who had witnessed Barry's departure from the centre had tracked Arthur down in his local pub close to the dispatch offices of the taxi firm. Arthur was fifty seven years old and nearly broke. Two marriages and one divorce, with another divorce on the cards due to his erratic and low paying hours meant Arthur was ripe for a deal.

Simon Kendall had approached him with the offer of another pint. Arthur was trying to make his current drink last as he knew he didn't have any more spare money this week. He also knew that if he didn't take home his pay packet unopened, he would be living in his car again. Simon's offer had been gratefully accepted and after another two pints Simon explained how Arthur could make a lot of money from this situation, and no one would ever know.

Arthur had been watching the news coverage about the patients since it all started weeks ago, like much of the country and the world, but he had been especially interested in learning how much money each of the awakened patients could make in the years to come. Arthur didn't really understand social media at all, and couldn't comprehend how people can make money from other people watching them, or things they had posted on line. Arthur hadn't joined the twenty first century, he was barely into the twentieth - his mobile phone, was basic, and made calls and sent and received texts. That was it, no video calling, no internet, nothing else.

In the taxi break room, the other drivers often compared their latest phones to each other, he just grunted. Recently one of the newer drivers had told Arthur, his phone was worth mega bucks because of its age. Apparently retro was the thing now, Arthur didn't care at all. Arthur did care however for the deal Simon Kendall had suggested. Simon had shown him a tiny camera and explained what he wanted Arthur to do. Simon wanted pictures and video of the patients and despite repeated calls to the centre, Simon like the rest of the media were swiftly brushed off. Simon however had a plan to get some footage of one of the patients, and on finding Arthur, he knew his plan could work.

Arthur was asked to allow Simon to place three of these cameras into his car before he went to collect the next discharged patient, and in exchange, Simon would give Arthur £3000 for each patient video he managed to bring back to Exeter. Arthur was aware that the other drivers at the firm, weren't interested in these fares, they preferred the shorter runs in and around the city. The taxi firm had agreed on rates with Arthur, and as he was willing, they had confirmed to him the previous day that he would be bringing back any other patients who wanted to return home to Exeter Simon didn't tell Arthur that he would be shadowing the car, as the range of the camera feed was less than a quarter mile.

Simon had tested the devices he had bought online, in his own car and was delighted by the quality of both the video feed and the photos he had got. Three days after Simon had put the cameras into Arthur's car, he got a call from Arthur confirming the next collection date. Simon and Arthur travelled back down to the Centre the following day. Simon had borrowed a friend's car so it wouldn't attract attention from the guards or security at the centre and was parked in a lay by waiting for Arthur and his passengers to come by.

Simon had been monitoring the feed on his mobile phone for an hour. Arthur had explained that there was a lot of security but they didn't check his car apart from for explosives, so Simon was sure the cameras would go unnoticed. Each of them looked like a button on the console of the car, and Simon had taken the precaution of switching them off remotely before Arthur had arrived at the main gate just in case they were monitoring signals. Arthur had arrived as expected, and after a short wait, he was allowed to drive onto the site and around to where Marilyn and Jacob were waiting.

Baz, Aiden, and Jimmy were sitting in the Ford Ka waiting for the trip to begin. Aiden had passed a bag of sweets around the car, and they were currently re-enacting the advert for the brand, speaking in silly child voices which made them sound like they were inhaling helium, which made Jacob smile as he heard them.

...His mates had been awesome, they had been there for him and his aunt all the way along, but now was the time for their lives to restart...

Marilyn was waiting in her wheelchair 'Doris' which Dr Mitchell had loaned her for the duration she needed it. Marilyn didn't refuse the chair as she knew the appearance of needing it fed into the story about her recovery and looked good. If she had walked down the corridor as she wanted to fit and well, that would have caused a lot of problems. She didn't need problems now she was close to leaving this place. She felt better than you had ever done, and that was down to the power of the dust and what it was. She didn't know consciously what the dust actually was but she knew that in return for her life, her services to help the others coming would be needed. She had felt calmer than ever before in her life, even those times travelling with her husband. She was ready, they all were.

As Arthur pulled up in his taxi, he smiled at the group and got out to get Marilyn into the back of the taxi. He was careful to make sure she sat on the side of the car that Simon had indicated to get the best pictures of her. Jacob got into the other side, and Arthur folded down the wheelchair and put it into the boot of his taxi. Baz, Aiden, and Jimmy were ready to go. Marilyn smiled at Dr Mitchell and her team who had come out to wave them off but she was glad to get away from her scrutiny. Arthur pulled away from the centre, and Baz's car followed behind through the large security cordon, and out onto the main road.

As the miles clocked up Arthur tried to engage Marilyn and Jacob in conversation as Simon had suggested. His last fare Barry had been very quiet during their trip home, and Arthur was careful this time not to be too nosy.

"So, are you feeling better, my dear?" Arthur asked brightly.

"Very much, thank you," said Marilyn stiffly. Jacob looked at his aunt curiously. She was normally a very gregarious lady who loved to chat. Perhaps her heart attack had taken its toll after all. Marilyn felt that something was wrong with this man, as she had realized that Dr Mitchell was suspicious or curious about the patients. She was aware that the world was desperately interested in all of them.

"The patients were the first people since Jesus to come back from the dead." Aiden had bashed Baz on the arm when he had said that, but Marilyn knew the media storm was only just beginning for all of them. She smiled at the rearview mirror where Arthur was smiling at her.

"Sorry, I'm not too chatty today, I'm just feeling a bit weary." She patted Jacob's arm. "I'm going to have a small nap, Jacob if that's OK?"

"Course it is," replied Jacob, and he put his arm around her shoulders so she could nest into him. Arthur watched the pair as Marilyn closed her eyes in sleep. He was furious but couldn't show it. Without footage, his £3000 was done for this trip. Simon wouldn't want two and half hour video of an old lady snoring her head off. He turned back to the road and concentrated on the route as he mused over what he could do about it.

A short distance behind the convoy, Simon was also fed up. He had placed a single listening device in the car unknown to Arthur so he could hear the conversation before he checked the video and picture footage later. When he heard Marilyn comment on her tiredness, he groaned out loud. He hadn't thought of that problem, and without at least some footage, he wasn't going to get any of the tabloids interested. As he listened he heard Arthur talk again.

"It's lovely to see how much you care for your auntie."

Jacob smiled at Arthur. "She's like another mum, her sister my mum lives in Canada, and when I got into the University she was nearly as proud as my parents were."

Arthur smiled. Bingo. If he couldn't get the old woman to talk, he could get the nephew to spill the beans on what's been going on. As the taxi carried on along the route back to their home, Jacob found himself talking easily to the nice driver. Marilyn was however not asleep. She hadn't been sure what this driver's angle was, but she was sure that something wasn't right. She continued to keep her eyes shut but she was listening intently to the information Jacob was giving over.

As Jacob continued to talk, she realized how worried Jacob and his friends all were about her. She yearned to tell him that she was fine, but she needed to appear to be what she wasn't, an elderly lady who had suffered a massive cardiac attack. However, when she heard the driver ask what had happened, she faked awakening and engaged Jacob in light conversation for the rest of the trip specifically discussing easy subjects such as when she could expect his friends to come over again for high tea. She could feel the driver was annoyed at her. He tried again a couple of times to engage her, but she just smiled and didn't reply.

As they arrived back in Exeter, she smiled at Jacob. "Nearly home," she said contently

He smiled back at her "Yes. Hoped for this day but didn't know if it would ever come."

Outside, Munstead Gardens fluttered a large white sheet with "WELCOME HOME MARILYN" written in black paint on it. It was held on the fence outside the sheltered complex with garden twine. Marilyn groaned internally she was sure Sue and Keith were behind that, possibly with the assistance of the on site staff. She smiled at the banner

"Something to do with you, Jacob?" she asked. He looked at the banner

"Maaaybe," he confirmed with a huge smile. "But the staff and your friends have missed you loads and wanted you to know how happy they all are you are home again. We too are all so thrilled you are home again." He looked worried "Too much?" She patted his hand again as the taxi drew up

"No, it's lovely thank you." Jacob looked relieved. Arthur parked the taxi in the visitor's car park so the cameras had a view out of the window towards the banner. He got out the wheelchair for Marilyn and helped her into it.

"Thank you." She smiled at him. "Very smooth journey, sent me off to sleep" Arthur smiled back but he looked worried. This lady was cannier than he had first thought.

...Did she know? Did she suspect what he was up to? No, she was a little old lady...

Arthur shook Jacob's hand and waved goodbye to them before he got back into his taxi and drove off to meet up with Simon at the local pub. As he left Marilyn looked back at the taxi frowning.

...Something was definitely up...the voice was warning her...

Jacob wheeled her into the reception area. Standing around waiting for her were Sue, Keith, and Lisa alongside her other friends. All of them were smiled broadly at her. Baz and the others were also there.

...They must have parked around the corner to be there before her. Baz was tearing up again. She did love him, all of them really. She gritted her teeth. At least the media hadn't discovered she was home yet....

She was badly mistaken.

* * *

Twenty minutes later Arthur was cradling his first pint of the evening. Simon had taken the pinhole cameras and the recorder out of the taxi and was watching the footage back with his headphones in. As he watched he occasionally made notes on a pad of paper beside him.

"Got some good stuff didn't I?" commented Arthur. He was still worried that it wasn't enough for the payment he had been promised.

"It's alright, but you were lucky the nephew decided to spill his guts before his aunt woke up. Some good stuff yes, but it would have been better if she had stayed awake." Simon shut off the recorder and put them and his phone and notepad back into his coat pocket. From the other one, he got out a small brown envelope and slid it across the table.

"£2000, for this one. When is your next trip booked for?"

Arthur shrugged as he slid the envelope off the table and into his jacket pocket. "There's only one patient left now I'm told and he hasn't been given the go ahead to leave yet, I was told by dispatch. They said they can give me a day's notice when they get the booking in."

Simon nodded his agreement. "OK, when you know we can meet again to get the cameras and equipment back in for the trip back." Simon got up from the table and left Arthur to contemplate his next trip to the centre, and how much money he could make from it.

Back at Munstead Gardens Marilyn was chatting to the other residents and staff. Baz Aiden and Jimmy had said goodbye to Marilyn with promises to come back the following week for tea. She had stood to hug each of them warmly and they had responded back. They had kept her nephew sane in this whole saga, and she was grateful for that. Jacob had stayed with her for the rest of the day. Lisa had made up the family room for him to stay with his aunt until she was settled back in.

As Jacob wheeled her back to her bungalow they chatted about the flower beds which were now starting to bloom again. He unlocked the door to her bungalow and pushed her inside. All of the bungalows at Munstead Gardens were suitable for wheelchair users, but Marilyn was not going to be using the chair for very long. Jacob pushed her into the living room and parked next to her "lift chair" as he called it.

The chair was designed to assist the person sitting in it to get back up, but Marilyn was always too busy to wait for the electrics to propel her upright and hoisted herself up more quickly than the chair could. Jacob helped her into the chair and went to make a cup of tea for them both. Marilyn leaned back in the chair and contemplated her surroundings.

Years of memories, from her marriage and travels with Jeremy, books, and ornaments all around her on shelves and in picture frames. As she looked at the picture of her beloved husband Jacob came back into the room with the tea and biscuits.

They sat and chatted for a while until Jacob noticed his aunt's eyes starting to close. "Right that's it, you are going for a nap now!" Marilyn concurred that was a good idea, and so he helped her into her bedroom for a nap and went to fetch his laptop from the family room so he could continue his studies whilst she slept. Marilyn lay on the bed and closed her eyes. ...

The man driving the taxi had disturbed me for some reason that I couldn't put my finger on why. He seemed nice enough to talk to but something inside her was telling her he was trouble. She didn't know what sort of trouble, but since she had awoken, the voices had not been wrong. They had told her how to behave, assured her that she would go home, and she would not be sick ever again. She trusted the voices and knew that she needed to be careful about that driver....

She was unaware of how true that feeling was until the following week.

* * *

Three days later Brian was cleared by Dr Mitchell to leave the centre. His COPD had not got better or worse, but he seemed brighter than when he had first arrived. His daughter and granddaughter had been keen for him to leave and Dr Mitchell had no clear reason for keeping him there. The taxi was booked for the following day to bring him back to the Home. He had been reluctant to go back there but his family home had been sold the year before to pay for his care, and he knew that Catherine was unable to look after him so back to the room without a view of the ocean it was.

Brian was also aware he was not as badly affected by the COPD as he had before he had come to the Centre, but like the others, he did not show any changes in his breathing issues whilst being tested. Like Marilyn, he accepted the offer of a wheelchair, but inside he also knew that he was starting to heal. He didn't understand how that was possible, but he knew it to be true.

Working in a pub for most of his adult life had caused this. Although he didn't smoke himself, he knew that his exposure to years and years of customers and staff smoking including the landlord he worked for was responsible for his illness. As COPD started to take effect in his fifties he realized what a horrible situation he was in. No chance of a transplant, just a horrible death, accompanied by increasingly regular bouts of chest pain and infection.

On arriving at the Ocean View Nursing home last year Brian had not expected to be around for very long. The restrictions on visiting hours, that horrible COVID and fears for his family had kept Brian alive despite all the suffering, and now he was going to be able to have a proper life.

He wasn't sure how that could happen, but he was healing. Brian had also heard the internal voice soon after awakening.

...At first, he feared he was going mad, but listening to the voice, he was calmed somehow. He realized he needed to continue to give the appearance of the man they saw on the outside, a man with a chronic lung condition. That was not the case though he realized. He was somehow better than he had been, and there were plans for him, for all of them, all that survived....

Catherine and Katie came into his room smiling at him and each other. He was thrilled to learn about Katie's plans for starting a nursing course next year. As he recovered he spent hours talking about Katie's grandmother, his precious Mary, and how she had spent her working life in the children's ward of the local hospital. Katie had been enthralled to hear about her Nana Mary.

Neither her mum nor her granddad had spoken much about her even when Katie had been doing a family tree project at school. She had learned later that her nana had been killed by a speeding driver in the city as she was getting off a bus to walk home. The driver had never been found, and Mary had been left to die in the street. Catherine had been her age at the time, and Brian had been forced to become a single father at a time when fathers didn't really do that, and with a job that meant long hours away from his family.

Despite all the obstacles and with the help and support of his family and friends, Brian had brought Catherine up to be a great person. Katie was so proud of her mum, and she hoped that by being a nurse, she could give back to the people who had helped her granddad to live again. Katie and Catherine helped Brian into the wheelchair, and after a final visit from Dr Mitchell, they went outside where Arthur Cook and his modified taxi were waiting to take them back to Exeter.

Arthur had received the call from the taxi control office two days earlier, and he had called Simon to arrange for the cameras to be fitted to his taxi that evening. After the fitting, Simon had offered to buy him another pint, and Arthur had accepted. Simon hadn't talked much about the earlier video Arthur had helped him make, only to say that there wasn't much on the video he could use, and this last one was going to be the money maker for both of them. Simon had instructed Arthur to make sure his air conditioning was on, so the patient wouldn't fall asleep, and if it was questioned to say that it was broken. Arthur knew this wasn't the reason why the old lady had slept, but he nodded his agreement and accepted another pint.

* * *

The following day Arthur had travelled back to the centre. Simon was in a hire car this time. He felt more paranoid each time he travelled back to the centre. He parked up in a different layby so he could join in behind Arthur's taxi when it went by. Arthur went through security as before and was waiting for his final load of passengers from the centre when they came out. Brian was helped into the taxi by Arthur and Catherine again into the spot previously used by Marilyn. Simon had confirmed this had been the best view of the patient and he was to do it again. Arthur placed Brian's wheelchair into the boot as Catherine and Katie loaded their bags into the boot beside it. They both then got into the other side of the taxi and belted up.

Arthur set off smoothly back through the security gate and onto the road. These passengers were far more animated than the last two Arthur thought with relief. The teenager had not stopped talking since she got in the car, commenting on the passing landscape, her future plans, and engaging her granddad in conversation. Arthur saw Simon parked up ahead of him but continued past without changing speed. He glanced in his rearview mirror and was glad to see Simon pull out into the light morning traffic.

After a few minutes, Arthur brightly asked the group, "Glad to be going home, I bet?"

Katie replied back confidently, "Yes, it's good to be going home with granddad!"

Bingo thought Arthur. Over the next two hours, Katie confided in Arthur some of the inside information about where they had been for the last few weeks. Arthur started by asking her if she was missing school, getting a typical teenage huff, but after asking her what she wanted to be when she grew up, he hit the bonus of hearing specific details. Katie had observed much activity in the centre and told Arthur how she wanted to be a nurse looking after people like her Nana. Neither the elderly gentleman whom Arthur knew was called Brian or his daughter had much to say for themselves but Catherine did add context to Katie's onrush of information. Arthur made sure he came over as sympathetic to their ordeal, asking polite questions which required more than a yes or no answer, having been briefed by Simon. He also gave them the impression he didn't really know who they all were, which endeared him to them.

Most of the staff working at the centre had also been less interested in their unique circumstances of being there than they were in making sure that each of the patients and their families were well looked after. As the centre was a military base, the professionalism of the staff had been appreciated by Catherine during her long wait for her dad to wake back up again. Being the last family to have their patient back again, Catherine had taken great comfort in the team who had cared for her father. She sat next to her father and held his hand. She never believed that she would be taking him back to Exeter, even if it was back to the hospice, but here he was sitting looking out at the passing countryside.

"Oh, Granddad I forgot to tell you. I had a zoom call with my careers advisor yesterday and he said that Bournemouth was a good choice for my nursing course. Mum and I are going down there next week for their careers fair."

Brian smiled at his only grandchild. "That's lovely to hear darling. You will do very well indeed."

Katie beamed at his comments. "It would be lovely if you could join us too.?"

Catherine glared at her daughter "Katie!"

"But Mum it would be lovely for granddad to see where I might be studying"

"Your granddad is still very ill love, you know that" Catherine gently admonished her daughter, but her heart was breaking too.

..It would be lovely for her Dad to see where his granddaughter was going to be staying for the next few years....

"I'll try chickie, no promises. My old lungs aren't good at the moment"

Inside, however, Brian knew that his lungs were actually starting to heal, and he might surprise his family in the end. As the journey continued Arthur asked Brian about who he'd be supporting in the upcoming football league matches. Brian confirmed he was supporting a north London team, who by coincidence Arthur also supported. For the rest of the journey Brian opened up to Arthur about past glories both for their team and also his life story, added to by Catherine and Katie.

In the hire car, behind them, Simon was delighted by the depth and breadth of the conversation that Arthur was managing to draw out of his passengers.

...This was more like it, real heartbreak in the middle - an elderly man not likely to see his granddaughter graduate. Better than some high rated American chat show host...

He smiled as the miles went by on their way back to Exeter.

* * *

Two hours later the taxi pulled up in the Ocean View Nursing Home's car park. As Brian was helped into the wheelchair by Arthur and his daughter, Mrs Bateman and Margaret came outside to welcome him back. Simon had parked up the road and was waiting for Arthur's taxi to appear.

"Welcome back, Mr Aykland," said Mrs Bateman stiffly. She had not been keen on receiving this patient back into her unit, due to the disruption his departure weeks ago had caused her. Catherine had spoken to the trustees of the home and Mrs Bateman had been instructed to welcome him back for as long as needed. The media vans had gone from the street now but her staff were still very disturbed by the events. Several of her more religious nurses and cleaners had decided to quit, and Mrs Bateman had been forced to help clean some of the rooms until she found more staff.

Brian looked at Mrs Bateman and felt her displeasure. He had never really liked the woman, even before this, but now he felt he could read her mind.

...She detests me, real hatred...

He smiled at her broadly and decided to make this fun.

"Couldn't kill me off, dear!" he said. Her shocked expression told him that he had hit home. "Back for another dose"

Catherine chuckled as she pushed her dad into the home.

"He's still in room six at the back of the unit," confirmed Margaret. "I'll be along in a moment to get him comfortable." She stopped to speak in a low whisper to Mrs Bateman. "He's going to be trouble."

Mrs Bateman nodded her agreement. "Watch him closely - any funny business and he's out." As Margaret walked off she nodded.

In room six, Brian was helped out of his wheelchair and into the chair by the bed. Katie went into the bathroom and stood on the toilet again.

"Same view of the ocean, granddad."

Brian chuckled. "Yes, chickie, they haven't moved it. Course if you go to live in Bournemouth, you will be by the sea all the time."

Katie got back down and went to hug Brian. "Don't worry about coming down to the University with us Granddad, I'll take loads of pictures and come and tell you all about it afterwards."

Brian hugged her back. "I'll try, chickie, but that's good as a backup."

Back in the car park Arthur got back into his taxi and drove off to meet with Simon and hand over the second trip footage. He saw Simon parked at the end of the street, and drove past him, Simon pulled out behind him and after ten minutes they were sat back at Arthur's favourite table with a pint each in front of them. Simon had taken the cameras out again and was looking back over the video feed on his mobile.

"Got a lot more this time didn't I?" commented Arthur as he took a large swig of his beer.

"Yes, much better," agreed Simon as he reached into his pocket and brought out another envelope.

"Shame it has to end," mused Arthur. He had liked being a spy for Simon and the pay was much better than driving cabs for a living. "If you have any other jobs like this, just let me know?" said Arthur.

"Will do," said Simon distractedly. "I need to get started on editing this. You have my pint if you like." As he stood up and shook Arthur's hand. Simon hurried out of the pub and back into his hire car. He had a lot of work to do.

* * *

20

Media frenzy

Two days later, Simon had finished editing the footage from both trips in Arthur's taxi and uploaded it to his video channel. He tipped off a friend working for a national newspaper that he had managed to get some footage, and within hours his channel became one of the most visited links in social media history.

Simon had been careful to edit the footage before uploading it to his channel, but it was clear that it had been taken without the consent of the people sitting in the back of the car.

Simon had checked in with a friend of his who was a solicitor who said that there could be issues of privacy citing the Human Rights Act of 1998, but it would take some time for any complaints to feed into a case in court. The backlog of criminal cases during lockdown had pushed other civil cases even further down the list, and in the meantime, Simon would be able to make a lot of money but his friend advised putting a lot of that away to defend his case.

Simon had established a social media channel some years earlier when he had first started working as a video journalist, but the highest view figures up to this week had been in the hundreds. He had done some investigations into the issues in the southwest including the lack of housing stock for locals and these videos were occasionally watched. The #sixnotdead had changed everything for him.

Within four hours of him uploading the footage from the journeys taken by Marilyn and Brian, he was becoming very wealthy indeed. The hosts of the channel had contacted him and asked him to become a partner which opened him up to the wonders of sponsored advertising before and after his videos played.

He didn't understand the specifics of it other than to work out on the back of his notebook, that he would make around 50p per 1000 views. The counter on the top of his laptop was turning over at a frantic rate and was in the millions already. He has been told that the range of potential sponsors to his channel was bigger than normal due to the unique nature of the videos.

An awful lot of people around the world of all ages, creeds, and religions were fascinated by the #sixnotdead and he was the first to bring any news of them. He realized he was going to be a very wealthy man.

* * *

Unfortunately, Arthur Cook has not fared as well. A call to the taxi office from Simon's friend working for the national newspapers had made Arthur's employers realize where the footage currently being viewed around the world had come from. They called Arthur into the office to find out if he was aware of the footage and his attitude had reinforced their belief that he was part of the deal. One of the most valuable contracts had come from the centre and they didn't want to prevent future work from being jeopardised. Arthur was immediately suspended subject to a disciplinary review with his union rep to support him later in the month.

He was furious at Simon. Someone must have told the firm about his deal, and he could only think Simon must have been the one who had done that to him. Unfortunately, he didn't have Simon's current mobile number and he didn't know where in the city he lived. Arthur had tried the only number Simon had given him but it was out of service. Arthur sat at his normal table in the pub nursing a beer. It was ten am, and he was now out of a job. The union rep wouldn't be able to help him, and his current wife would throw a fit when she realized that he was out of work again. As he drank he got more and more depressed.

...A measly £5000 for what was going to likely be my last proper job...

Arthur thought back over the events. He had seen some of the footage which was picked up by several news channels earlier in the week, but he hadn't seen anything that had pointed to him till the very end.

A clear shot of him helping Marilyn out of the taxi into her wheelchair and wheeling her to the front door.

...That's what had done it for me...

His bosses at the taxi company had been very clear when they had hired him that some of their customers might be well known celebrities. This part of Devon attracted the great and the good to their second homes, and so his employers needed to make sure that he wasn't gossiping about them. All of the drivers had signed agreements to that effect including him, but he had forgotten about that until he had been called back in. Now he was screwed, and there was nothing he could do about it.

* * *

The Ocean View Nursing Home was bombarded by calls from media outlets all wanting to speak to the patient who was one of the #sixnotdead. Mrs Bateman fielded most of the calls for the first hour but in the end, she decided to switch off the telephone system. Families of the other residents then started calling her personal mobile for updates as to the state of their family members and whether they were being disturbed by all the frenzy.

The news story brought several media vans which then clogged up the road outside the home. Mrs Bateman called the police to move them on, and eventually, a corral for them was set up in a small cul de sac behind the home. The residents of the local area were delighted to see Mrs Bateman frustratedly trying to get by the vans as she left work for the day. She had made their lives a misery ever since she started working there. The previous home manager had been part of their community but they were sure that Mrs Bateman had been behind several of the residents getting parking fines. The other residents of the Ocean View Nursing Home also enjoyed the frenzy outside.

Brian had not come out to speak to any of them, he spent the time in his room reading and watching TV. Catherine had called Brian frantically on hearing the news from Katie who had seen the video first. Katie's friends had spotted them in the video and had tagged Katie on a social media link. Brian had been calm and practical on the phone. He told Catherine to not comment on the story and to just hunker down. He made her laugh by adding that some half-baked celebrity doing something strange would push them off the top spot before too long

* * *

Munstead Gardens off Paris Street was also besieged by media as the location Marilyn had been taken to was clearly seen on screen thanks to Arthur's careful parking at the end of the video. Marilyn declined to speak to any of the reporters by phone or in person, and Jacob, Baz, Jimmy, and Aiden also declined with a smile and shake of the head as they arrived for the first of the afternoon tea's Marilyn had promised them. Lisa the Warden politely explained that

"The patient would not be speaking to any media and can they please stop trampling the begonias in the front garden."

Eventually, the reporters left, and peace was restored to the quiet complex.

Inside her bungalow, Marilyn was hosting a social with 'her boys'. She was grateful for their loyalty during the whole horrible time.

"I would like to take you all away on holiday, my treat!" Marilyn announced as Baz passed her the plate of biscuits. Jacob and the others looked startled.

"But Auntie Marilyn, you've only just got home" spluttered Jacob.

"All the more reason to get away," Marilyn replied. "A little sea air I think - I've always loved Eastbourne; Jeremy and I loved that place when we weren't flying all over the world. I thought we might both retire there, but no" she added sadly. "One more visit - please?" she implored.

Jacob smiled. "Of course, Auntie, with all of us?"

"Yes, you boys have been so good to me, a few days away during your summer holidays would make me very happy indeed." Marilyn added, "My friends Sue and Keith have 'the internet' so they can help me make the bookings.

Baz added, "Aiden, Jimmy, and I can go in our car."

"And I will arrange a nice hire car for Jacob to drive me down in style," smiled Marilyn. Jacob blushed. He knew that Marilyn found his old car very uncomfortable and since it failed his MOT he had been borrowing cars for trips he needed to make. She patted his hand. "You've made an old lady very happy."

Inside a secure part of the Army Medical Centre, news had reached the security forces of the videos produced by Simon Kendall. Wing Commander Cooke was asked if the journalist who had leaked the video should be brought in for questioning. After some discussion, the consensus was to watch and wait.

None of the patients had been forbidden from talking to the media but Dr Mitchell had advised them all not to. It had been decided not to place surveillance on any of the patients as the media were likely to spot anything like that. The patient's calls and other communications were being monitored, but unfortunately, that was not how the patients were communicating.

* * *

21

Planning

As the media frenzy started to ease, each of the #sixnotdead heard the same voice in their heads. The message was the same to each of them.

...They needed to come to the same location. The original point that the dust had landed in. They all needed to collect some of the pebbles that had landed and spread the dust further around the country. Without further spread, the dust could not continue to grow, and each of them had committed to do their part. The dust had saved them all, and they were needed for the next step...they probably were being watched so they all had to be very careful about how and when they went to retrieve their pebbles...

None of the six had felt any reservations about what they were doing. All of them earnestly felt that they were obligated to help the dust spread. None of them would have lived without it, and none of them felt obligated to alert the authorities including Dr Mitchell to what was happening to them, and how they were helping the dust to spread further.

They were all aware that parts of the Government had been keen to hold them for security reasons. As they were freely giving their assistance to something sentient and something not of this world, they all feared they and their families could be held indefinitely and studied. None of them was prepared to take that risk, and all of them had been told by the voices that once they had gone and spread the dust they would all be left alone to enjoy their remaining lives. They needed to get back to their normal habits in order to allay the fears of the authorities.

* * *

Barry was the first to go to the location. He had a legitimate reason for being on the golf course near to where the pebbles had landed, as he had played there before. Barry knew that his friend Chester was always up for a game, so after making a call in which he challenged his friend to beat "an old sparking sparkie" which gained roars of approval from Chester, they arranged to meet for a game in a couple of days. Chester had been unsure whether his mate would still have a rough sense of humour, but he was heartened when two days later Barry was waiting to tee off.

Barry knew where the dust had fallen and as they played around Barry was enjoying his first trip out with his golfing buddy. He didn't have to fake his enjoyment of being out on the course again. As they got to the hole nearest the dust Barry faked a bad shot that sent his ball over into the woodlands. Chester went into fits of laughter and sent Barry off to get his ball.

Barry huffed as he went to retrieve his ball which he had deliberately shot into the location. He heard the voice told him he would find what he was looking for.

..In that brush over there...

Half buried in the ground were grey smooth pebbles, but Barry knew that these weren't from Earth. He picked one up carefully and cradled it in his hand. It started to vibrate softly. He knew it felt the dust within him and his dust felt the dust the pebbles were made of. He picked up a handful of the pebbles and put them all into his jacket pocket.

Just as Chester came into the woods to look for him, Barry found his ball and allowed Chester more ribbing. He played on knowing that others would come for the rest.

When Barry got home, he kissed Maisie full on the lips. His kids groaned but he didn't care.

"I fancy a holiday!" he declared. "Reckon all of us are owed one after the year we have had"

Maisie looked up at him. "Can we afford it?"

"Not looking for anything abroad, too much hassle but there is Cumbria," Barry declared. "Your mum and I had a lovely honeymoon there" as he pinched her bum to more groans from Hugo Mark and Ryan

"Daaad!" they chorused.

"Too much information, Dad," said Hugo solemnly.

237

"It's a great place for a holiday, water sports, loads of lovely cows, country walks," Barry chuckled. "I'll take a look tonight on the internet. The first week of the summer holidays?" he asked Maisie who nodded.

As he went upstairs with his golf bag he took out the pebbles and put them inside his golf bag until he needed them. Golfing in Cumbria, he was sure there was a nice course up there and if not one of those romantic strolls around a lake. He hummed as he put his golf kit away.

* * *

Jed went next, he took a bus into the suburb where the golf course was and got off at a stop just down from the golf course entrance. As he walked along the road, several luxury cars left the golf course car park and one driver glared at him as they passed on the road. Jed ignored them and walked down until he got to a woodland path just past the turning. Jed had a dog lead with him for cover, and if challenged he would tell them that his dog had run off. He had found the lead in a bin near to his new home, and although it was broken it would do. Jed walked down the path swinging the dog lead as he went and following the acorn signs which indicated the way that would eventually lead to the hospital.

He walked for a few minutes enjoying the fresh air and the woodland path until he heard the voice

...Stop here, get off the path, go up the bank...

Jed climbed the bank and as he got to the top he could see the golf course over to the left. Jed carefully made his way around the tree line until he too came to the spot recently found by Barry.

...Here...

He bent down and brushed his hand over the soft leaf strewn earth until he found what he was looking for. He picked up several more of the pebbles and put them all into his pocket. He then made his way back onto the path and turned back the way he came. Jed was feeling very good.

Mr C was going to be surprised to see him, but Mr C would regret trying to kill him

* * *

Jed managed to stay away from Mr C for nearly a month after he returned to Exeter. He hadn't lied to Mr Tenson or Kitty. He had done with drugs, and without any side effects from coming off them, and that he knew was down to the dust. He was better than he had ever been and now was his chance to make things right for him and Kitty. Jed waited until the end of the quietest night at the casino to make his move. He had worn his most tatty anorak but inside the pocket was his revenge. One of the pebbles that had fallen weeks ago was inside and he knew that the dust would help him take that revenge. The voice had told him what he needed to do

....hold the pebble...let it crumble in your pocket then shake his hand....

Jed walked up the road, passing the small number of students who made this part of the city their playground at night. He went around a particularly loud group who were chanting as they walked, but they didn't cause him any trouble.

Jed walked into the lobby of the casino and nodded at Kevin who was the doorman as well as a heavy when Mr C went on one of his 'teaching' visits. Jed knew what those visits really mean. Usually ending up in the local A & E, but Jed had heard about one mouthy addict who had ended up in the local river with head injuries. His corpse was fished out a few days later.

"Come to see Mr C please," Jed said in a sad voice. He wasn't going to act as he felt. Kevin nodded and picked up a phone on the wall. "Jed's here to see you Mr C." Kevin nodded and put the phone back on the wall. "Go through, he's at the bar"

Jed nodded again and shuffled through to the bar area. The casino was one of Mr C's legitimate businesses but its decor came purely from the proceeds of crime.

...It was like something out of Vegas...

Jed thought.

...I've never been to Vegas, or anywhere out of the UK, perhaps that could now change? ...

As Jed came into the room, he saw Mr C sat on one of the decorative bar stools. Mr C turned to face him. Jed realized that Mr C was scared, he could feel his panic, but to look at him, he seemed calm and composed.

...He's frightened of you, Jed. You shouldn't have lived...

"Hello Jed, are you feeling better?"

"Yes thanks, Mr C. Don't know what happened to me."

"It was a purer product but shouldn't have caused any issues. I must have a word with my chemist and see what they can find." Mr C turned back to the bar "Would you like a drink, Jed?"

"No thanks, Mr C, I just wanted to come by and let you know I was OK."

Mr C nodded and said, "So what are your plans now?"

Jed replied, "Well I think Kitty and I are going on holiday first, then I'm not sure."

Mr C paused and turned back "Holiday eh? Whereabouts?"

"London I think, Kitty's lived in outer London when I met her and I want to show her all the sights. Neither of us had been tourists during our time there. No point trying to book somewhere abroad this year."

Mr C nodded again. "OK, well hope you are feeling better soon."

Jed paused, put his hand inside his pocket feeling the pebble vibrate violently and crumble, and then turned back to Mr C "Just wanted to say thank you, Mr C, for all you have done for Kitty and me" he held out his hand. Mr C looked at his hand for a moment then grasped it with both of his hands.

"Good luck Jed, see you soon" Kevin came back into the room as Jed was leaving, Jed could see in the mirror in front of him Mr C nodding to Kevin, which meant that he was going to be able to leave.

"Kevin will see you out now" Jed nodded and shuffled back outside onto the street. His pocket had the remains of the pebble inside it which had turned to dust. As he walked through the streets back to his new flat he occasionally lifted a small handful out and dropped it down onto the street and pavements, the dust fell and sparkled in the late evening sunshine. No one noticed, he hummed as he walked and sprinkled more dust around the city.

* * *

Two days later Mr C succumbed to a massive coronary attack whilst entertaining his latest lady friend in his apartment above the casino. Jed's visit two days earlier was not suspected as being the cause, but Jed knew that the dust he had transferred to Mr C's hand had infected his heart and would have caused the heart attack.

Mr C staggered out of the bed clutching his chest, as the dust caused multiple blockages to his arteries. His heart stopped as did his breathing. Mr C's companion Rose quickly called down to the casino and as Kevin dashed upstairs, she called for an ambulance.

Kevin looked around and yelled at her "Get that stuff off the desk!"

Rose turned and swept the cocaine back into its packet and into the drawer. Kevin started CPR but Mr C was gone. As the paramedics arrived and started to work on his boss, Kevin stood up and went over to Rose.

"What happened? Was he doing some of that?" Kevin indicated the desk where Rose had hidden the cocaine.

"No," she replied tearfully. "He was off that, didn't like how it made him perform." She blushed.

"Put some clothes on woman," Kevin barked before turning to the paramedics who were still working on his boss.

The senior paramedic said, "I'm sorry - time of death 12.23 am."

Rose sobbed as Kevin came over to them. "Fix him!" he growled menacingly

"I'm sorry Sir but he's gone, no heartbeat, no breathing and his pupils are fixed and dilated. We will transport him to the hospital to have the doctor confirm death." said the senior paramedic.

He stood up and stared at Kevin calmly. Kevin looked at him but then turned away. "I need to call some people." As the paramedics put Mr C onto a stretcher to take him to the hospital Kevin made the first of many calls to his boss's network.

* * *

Samir made the journey back to Exeter the following day by train, telling Tamir that he needed to go and collect some of his belongings. Tamir had offered Samir a room in his house in Manchester and Samir had also decided that he was going to start training to become a vet, which he could do at Manchester University. Tamir had helped Samir since he had come back to Manchester and Samir knew that his life was now in Manchester and not in Exeter.

Unfortunately, Tamir was on a long shift pattern for several weeks and couldn't drive his cousin back to his home. Samir wasn't upset at coming back. He too had heard the voice

...You need to collect something, give it to the others that can't go, spread the dust in your new home...

Samir got off the train after four hours and one change at Birmingham and stood on the platform breathing in the fresh air. He shifted his borrowed rucksack more comfortably on his back, he realized he was actually going to miss this city.

Samir walked to the station exit and handed over his ticket to the inspector who glanced at him suspiciously. Samir was used to these reactions, a mixed race man with a rucksack. "Nothing in there, mate!" he said, jostling the rucksack around.

The inspector looked shocked but didn't comment. Samir walked out of the station and caught the H2 bus from down the road. He sat on one of the seats at the back of the bus and watched the pedestrians and traffic. As he got off at the stop nearest his family shop, he stopped on the pavement and looked across at the shop which had been his home all of his life.

His father and mother had come to the UK in the 1970s and had worked long hours to make a life here. The shop was open again, which Samir was glad of. He knew his father needed to work, and without an income, he couldn't afford to pay the rent on the flat upstairs. Samir took a deep breath and walked across to the shop door. As he went inside he saw that the shop was empty

...A blessing. No nosy neighbours or customers to be gawked at...

His father was stacking shelves in the back of the shop.

"Hi Dad," Samir said softly. His father startled and turned around. His face lost all colour

"Sammi, what are you doing here? Where is Tamir, did he bring you down?"

Samir's father looked around for his nephew. Samir realized he could feel his father's disappointment that his favourite relative wasn't there.

...He doesn't want me, he wants a son like Tamir...

"Tamir's working, Dad, but I'm here to collect my stuff. He's offered me a room in his house, and I have decided to go to university to become a vet." Samir looked at his father steadily.

"But this is your home Samir, you need to be here with us" Mr Azmed implored "We need you."

Samir looked at his father sadly "No Dad, I need to be away from here. You don't need me around, the shop's had enough gawkers..." he trailed off. Samir turned and walked to the stairs behind the counter.

"Your mother is at the mosque."

Samir nodded that he understood and walked up the stairs to his room to pack his life away for a new one in Manchester. Samir packed his rucksack and went back down into the shop. His dad was standing by the counter waiting for him. "Goodbye, Dad."

Mr Azmed hugged him fiercely and let him go. "Keep in touch?"

"Yes, I will." But Samir knew that this was a lie. Samir walked out of the shop for the last time in his life. Samir took a deep breath.

* * *

Now for the second part of his trip. He walked south of his family shop through comfortable suburbs until he reached the other end of the woodland path Jed had been on days earlier.

...walk down this path...

Samir hoisted his rucksack again and walked down the path until he reached the same point as Jed. Samir took off his rucksack and stashed it behind a large hedge to the left of the path.

...climb up here...

He then climbed up onto the ridge and walked along until he too found the spot where the grey pebbles had landed. He collected all the remaining pebbles and put them into his jacket pocket. He would be handing them over discreetly in the city later today to the others who couldn't come to collect some themselves. He walked back to the ridge and climbed back down, retrieving his rucksack from behind the hedge.

He walked back to Topsham Lane and caught a bus back to the Railway Station. The first part was now done. Samir walked to the left luggage centre in the Station and bought a space for the rest of the day. Once free of his rucksack, Samir strolled around the city saying goodbye to some of the places he had loved when he was living there. He sat on a bench for a while in Cathedral Green watching the tourists milling around.

As he sat there, he spotted the first person he was to meet. Marilyn was coming towards him on a mobility scooter, and she was on her own.

...She looked radiant, not sick at all...

Samir thought. Samir had never met her before, but he realized who she was as soon as she smiled at him. She stopped the scooter and said

"Hello, could you tell me the time please?"

Samir smiled broadly and pointed up to the Astronomical Clock on the side of the Cathedral "No good looking at that - it's half past one."

Marilyn smiled and patted his hand, and as she did so he popped several of the pebbles into her cardigan pocket. No one spotted the move which was hidden by her arm.

She smiled more broadly at him and said "Well I must be off, I am having tea with my nephew in that cafe and I can't be late. we're going off for a few days to Eastbourne" Samir smiled at her as she turned her scooter expertly around and headed for the cafe where Jacob was waiting for her.

Ten minutes later Joshua walked around the corner onto the green. He sat down at the other end of the bench from Samir. Neither of them acknowledged each other but they were keenly aware that the voices had calmed down for both of them.

...*this is the one*....

Joshua stood up and as he did so, Samir dropped a packet on the floor.

"This yours mate?" he asked Joshua indicating the packet.

"Oh thanks, yes it fell out of my pocket" replied Joshua with a grin. He picked up the packet, nodded to Samir, and went on his way back home.

Samir had one more delivery to do, and this would be more complicated, but he had a plan. He walked back toward the station but stopped off to pick up some of the supplies he would need. He walked down to the final location and stopped across the road from a tall Georgian building with a large sign planted in the car park adjacent to it 'Ocean View Nursing Home & Hospice (part of the Homes2Homes Group)'

Samir smiled as he walked across the road. He held a clipboard in his hand to which was attached a large envelope with 'Mr Brian Aykland Private and Confidential' and 'By hand' written in large capital letters on it. Samir had filled the envelope with random leaflets and hidden inside there was a small clear plastic bag filled with the remaining pebbles. He walked confidently to the reception area on the ground floor where a young woman with 'Rachel, Receptionist' badge pinned to her uniform was sitting behind the desk.

"Good afternoon," said Samir "I'm from Russell and Nursley the Solicitors. I have a 'by hand' envelope to deliver, please."

"Who is it for?" asked the receptionist "A Mr Brian Aykland" replied Samir glancing at his clipboard. "It's to do with his revised will but I need to deliver it in person to him"

Rachel looked at her register. "He's in room six but I have a note stating no visitors apart from close family. You can give it to me."

"I'm sorry it's got to be handed directly to him," replied Samir. "More than my job's worth, I've only worked there for a month."

Rachel looked at Samir and he tried to look regretful.

"The manager is on lunch. I suppose as long as you are quick, down the corridor on the right there." Rachel pointed to the back of the reception," the last door on the right hand side"

"Thanks!" said Samir "Appreciate it" as he walked down following her instructions. He knocked on the last door on the right.

"Come in," said a frail voice. Samir opened the door. Brian was sitting in a comfortable chair near the window. Brian smiled broadly as Samir came in.

"I wondered how you were going to get past the miserable old bird."

"I appealed to the mercy of the receptionist - Rachel is it?"

"Yeah, she is nice, one of the good ones." Samir handed over the envelope.

"They're in there?" Brian said.

"Yes a few" replied Samir

"I'm going to take my daughter and granddaughter to Bournemouth next week. Katie is going to be a nurse."

"Nice location," said Samir. "I'd better go before the manager gets back."

He shook Brian's hand and said, "Goodbye" and walked back down to the reception. As he came into the room he saw the receptionist blanch. Beside her was a stern looking woman who must be the manager Rachel mentioned earlier and Brian had called a miserable old bird.

"And who are you, and why have you been in our patients' corridors?" asked Mrs Bateman sternly.

"Delivering legal documents to our client," replied Samir who still has his clipboard waving it at her.

"And who is your client?" asked Mrs Bateman stiffly

"It's confidential, sorry," replied Samir "Thanks for your assistance Rachel" he added waving at her as he left the building.

Mrs Bateman glared at his departing figure. "Who was he here to see?" she barked at Rachel.

"Mr Aykland," replied Rachel meekly Mrs Bateman marched down to Brian's room and banged on the door

"Come in," said Brian. Mrs Bateman barrelled into the room closely followed by Rachel who looked mortified.

"Hello, Mrs Bateman. Looking more lovely than ever, how are you?" Brian asked cheerfully "And the beautiful Rachel." Rachel blushed and shuffled her feet standing behind Mrs Bateman.

Mrs Bateman was nonplussed. "Did you have an unauthorised visitor just now?" she asked

"I had an authorised visitor, yes, a courier from my solicitors," replied Brian "He was bringing me a copy of my documents." Mrs Bateman looked unsettled.

"Was there anything else, Mrs Bateman? Only my bowels require some urgent action." Brian smiled cheekily.

Mrs Bateman turned without speaking and ushered Rachel out too.

Brian had hidden the pebbles inside his security box under the bed, and he had the only key on a chain around his head. He knew that Mrs Bateman would come looking for evidence of wrongdoing but Brian was ahead of her and before a short time the pebbles would be gone. He smiled. His daughter was coming in this afternoon, and he had some good news to give her.

* * *

Samir strolled back to the railway station. The mission was completed in Exeter, now he was going onto a new and better life up in Manchester. He walked into the storage area, picked up his rucksack, and caught the next train back to his new home. As it left Exeter Samir took a deep breath of the fresh air. He was going to miss this place.

* * *

22

#sixaliveagain

Maisie didn't think she had ever been happier in her life, bar having her kids and marrying Barry. She was sat at a small cafe on the shoreline of Lake Windermere sipping from a cup of coffee in the shade of a parasol. The sun felt warm on her legs and a light breeze added to the feeling of contentment.

Across the pier Barry, Hugo Mark and Ryan were all sat listening to the paddleboard instructor who was explaining how they should sit on the board and what to do if they come off in the water. Barry looked over at Maisie and winked at her as he wiggled his butt towards her.

...He was a very handsome man even togged up in a wetsuit, though it did make him look a bit like a seal...

His electric shock wound on his leg was healing well, and there didn't appear to be any other issues. She had her Barry back and she couldn't stop smiling.

The boys were loving the paddleboarding experience, none of them had ever done anything like this before, and it was a great bonding opportunity for Barry and his children.

Maisie and Barry had located the paddleboard centre earlier in the week when Barry had suggested a romantic walk around the lake. The boys had been engrossed in brochures of other activities lying on their beds, and bickering on which of them was brave enough to try the abseiling out without vomiting. Maisie and Barry had walked most of the way around the south side of the lake, with the smooth waters being ruffled as boats and other craft went by. They lay down on a small patch of grass next to the shoreline and talked about their future together. Eventually, Maisie fell asleep, the fresh air and two glasses of wine at lunch had lulled her into slumber. This was the first part of Barry's plan.

Barry had waited until Maisie was fully asleep before he had walked for a short distance around the shoreline emptying out his pocket which had held the pebbles. As he had held them, they had vibrated as they had done for Samir and crumbled into dust. The wind was blowing from the shoreline out across the water, so Barry had held his hand up and dust had blown onto the lake. He walked back to where Maisie was still sleeping. Barry leaned over and kissed her until she woke up.

"Oh dear, I am a lightweight." she scoffed.

"They were large glasses of wine" Barry admitted. She punched him in the arm as he said."I think there is a paddleboard hire place a bit further on. Do you think the boys would like that?"

Maisie agreed and they had booked the places on the way back to the hotel. Unseen by Maisie Barry had deposited more of the dust around the pier as Maisie was talking to the receptionist of the paddleboard company.

He had trampled it into the ground around the pier walkway discreetly like a soldier in one of the escape war movies his dad had been keen on. Barry had loved watching these films with his dad who had been a small child when World War Two had started.

One film, in particular, came back to Barry now, that of prisoners of war using socks inside their trousers to hide the soil they were digging out under the barracks they were forced to live in. Barry had used the same trick by cutting a hole in one pocket of his jacket inside the lining so he could poke dust out if people were watching. He looked around him and saw that no one was interested in anything he was doing, and so he sat on the pier and added handfuls of dust to the dirt path beside him. As Maisie had come out Barry heard the voice

...*your role is now done, enjoy your life...*

He smiled and ran towards her like something out of a romance novel with a goofy grin on his face and his arms outstretched towards her. This resulted in further giggles from Maisie. Barry loved to hear his wife giggle.

He was a very lucky man, and he would never ever forget that now.

Maisie had been happy to watch her family enjoying the time together, she didn't really like water sports. Barry and the boys had a great afternoon on the water, and all of them eventually managed to stay on their boards without effort. When their time was up, they all came back tired and hungry to join her. As the boys demolished piles of sandwiches and hot chocolate Maisie looked over at Barry with pride and enormous love. He gazed back at her and smiled.

* * *

Joshua picked up the hire car arranged by Sue and Keith the following week. Marilyn had just smiled when he asked what car they were having. She gave him the address and the details of when to pick the car up. At ten am Joshua walked into the car hire reception and gave his details. He passed over his driving license and signed the paperwork. The receptionist handed over the keys and directed him to a sleek blue Jaguar parked next to the door. Jacob gawked. It was a beautiful car. He got in and started it. The receptionist explained the features of the car and wished him a good trip. Jacob carefully exited the car park and drove around to Munstead Gardens where he parked in one of the visitor's spaces.

Keith came out of his bungalow and walked over to where Jacob was admiring the lines of the car.

"Your aunt wanted something special, think she got it!" he said. "That's a beautiful car." Jacob nodded. As they stood there Baz drove up in his car and whistled at Jacob.

"Wowzers man, that is gorgeous." Aiden & Jimmy both got out of Baz's car and walked around admiring the shape and the gadgets inside. Baz tried to open the bonnet to look inside but Marilyn came out in her wheelchair pushed by her neighbour Sue and Baz retreated back to his car.

"We all ready?" Marilyn asked

"Yep, all set," replied Baz.

Jacob helped his aunt to the Jaguar and settled her in the passenger seat, adding her bag to his in the boot before getting behind the wheel. He set the GPS for Eastbourne avoiding motorways, he wanted his aunt to enjoy the countryside, as he feared this might be her last ever trip away. He'd already agreed on the route with Baz a few days later pouring over route maps of the area between Exeter and Eastbourne. They had agreed on a route that would take them longer but would be more pleasant to travel and scenic for Marilyn.

The hotel that Keith and Sue had booked for them using Marilyn's credit card was one of the more luxurious ones in Eastbourne. Baz and some of his fellow students had come to Eastbourne for a stag party a couple of years ago but their accommodation was much less luxurious and at the other end of the town. A break for lunch was agreed at the half way point just outside Southampton at a local pub. Marilyn appeared to be thoroughly enjoying the whole experience and managed a large cheese sandwich and coffee, which surprised and delighted Jacob and his friends. She had brightened considerably as the miles clicked by, regaling Jacob with stories of her trips to Eastbourne with his Uncle Jeremy whom Jacob had barely known.

Jacob had only come to England when he had got his place at University and had lived in Canada for most of his life before that. He had seen pictures of his aunt and uncle on their trips around the world. Jacob's parents hadn't really travelled much before they moved to Canada, and Jacob had been the only one of their children who yearned to travel. He had thought about his life after university and had decided he wanted to live somewhere other than Canada for a few years, and whilst his aunt was alive, he wanted to spend as much time with her as possible. To have her adore his friends was a bonus to him and them, and this trip had been a welcome distraction for all of them.

As the party arrived in Eastbourne the GPS directed them to the hotel and the car park behind. Jacob carefully parked the Jaguar, and Baz then parked his rust ridden old vehicle behind it. The car park attendant came over and glared at Baz.

" Do you have a reservation at this hotel, Sir?" Marilyn wound down the window of the Jaguar and addressed the attendant.

"Yes young man, I have reserved five rooms at this hotel. Do you not want us here?" she asked coolly.

The attendant blanched and apologised and quickly helped Marilyn out of the car and into her wheelchair. Baz, Jimmy, and Aiden sniggered as the attendant's ears got more and more flushed, but stopped as Jacob glared at them. The attendant ushered the party into the reception area from the wheelchair entrance and went to collect their bags.

"Marilyn Francis and party" Marilyn announced as the receptionist peered over at her.

"Ah, Mrs Francis. Lovely to see you all," said the receptionist who had a badge proclaiming, "I'm Hector - ask me for anything!" which caused Baz to snigger and nudge Jimmy in the ribs. Jacob glared at Baz again, but Marilyn smiled. She was having a lovely time. Hector swiftly checked them all in and issued car passes for both cars. The bags were taken up to their rooms which overlooked the pier and beach.

Each of the rooms had more space than any of the
students had seen before and despite more glares from
Jacob, Baz Jimmy and Aiden jumped on each of their
beds to "test them out." Marilyn was in a ground floor
room for better access and this came with a walk in
shower and facilities. Jacob was in the room adjacent to
hers, so he could be on call if she needed help. Plans had
been made to have dinner in a local restaurant that Sue
had booked for them that evening. Marilyn asked Jacob
if he could take her out in her wheelchair that afternoon
before dinner so she could look at the sea. Jacob agreed
and after making sure Marilyn had her jacket and bag,
they went along the seafront for a while watching the
passing tourists and locals out for a walk in the fresh air.
As they got to the pier, Marilyn asked Jacob to stop so
she could admire the view. He parked her wheelchair
adjacent to a park bench and sat down next to her.

"This is really lovely Jacob, thank you for coming with me,
and thank you to your friends too. I know Eastbourne is
a bit old fashioned, but your Uncle Jeremy loved it here,
and it is comforting for me to be here too."

Jacob smiled. "It is entirely our pleasure Auntie Marilyn,
You really are very generous to us all. I don't think Baz
and the others are going to want to be going back to
their student digs after staying here"

Marilyn chuckled. "Probably not, but they have been so supportive to you." Jacob looked at his phone that had just started to ring

"Baz," he said

"Go take it," replied Marilyn. "I'm fine here, just enjoying the beautiful view" Jacob answered the phone moving away to get a better signal and as he did so, Marilyn reached into her pocket and held onto a pebble which she felt vibrate and crumble in her hand.

As she withdrew the crumbled dust she slid her hand down the side of the wheelchair away from Jacob and released the dust onto the ground, where it sparkled and blew away in the light breeze. She looked over to Jacob who was engrossed in his call and repeated the same process with the next pebble. As she was reaching for the third pebble she felt Jacob return so took her hand out of the pocket and placed it back on her handbag on her lap.

"Is Baz OK?" she asked

"He's fine, just worried he didn't bring enough underpants with him for this trip and wondered if it was OK to ask in the hotel where he could buy some from," Jacob replied

"Oh bless him!" said Marilyn as she chuckled. Jacob joined in and pushed her back to the hotel to get ready for dinner.

Dinner was arranged at a local Turkish restaurant in the centre of the town, which Marilyn had visited with her husband before his death. The restaurant was tiny and very busy but the party had arranged for a table before arriving. The food was cooked in front of them, and after several glasses of wine, Jacob was enjoying the atmosphere.

Marilyn managed another huge portion of food and a glass of wine during the meal and was gently encouraged to try some of the more interesting items on the menu.

Baz and Aidan had never tried this type of food before but were guided by the owner to items that they would enjoy. Jimmy had experienced a lot of ethnic food as he came from Leeds, and he also helped his friends to choose foods that they would enjoy.

"It's not a contest to see who is going to eat the most food!" Jimmy chided Baz and Aiden. "It's all about flavour here." By the end of the meal, all had declared this restaurant a success.

As they walked back to the hotel, Jacob pushing Marilyn in 'Doris' her wheelchair, she was smiling again.

...this trip had been a huge success and they would be travelling around the area for a couple of days so she had plenty of time to drop more dust around....

* * *

The following day after breakfast Marilyn asked that they take her to St Leonards for a push along the seafront. Jacob and Jimmy volunteered with Baz and Aiden deciding to stay in Eastbourne and check out the local pubs. A football match was scheduled and Jacob knew that Baz was desperate to see his team's match on a pub's TV set. Marilyn was happy to let the group split up, and so the group departed for St Leonard's using the Jaguar, and Baz and Aiden walking down to the town to find a pub showing the football. Marilyn sat in the passenger seat again and Jimmy was in the back with Jacob driving. Jimmy waved at some tourists as they drove along the seafront with several gawking thinking he was a celebrity off on holiday. This caused great amusement in the car with Marilyn bursting into fits of giggles as each group peered into the car to see who was in there.

As they arrived in St Leonards Jimmy directed them to a good car park near to the seafront. Jacob and Jimmy helped Marilyn out of the car into 'Doris' her wheelchair and alternated pushing her along with admiring the seafront houses. As they approached Hastings pier, Marilyn put her hand up

"Could you push me along the pier boys? The original pier was where your Uncle proposed to me, and also where I scattered his ashes. This one isn't as nice as the original but it's still dear to me" Jacob and Jimmy agreed and so they set off for the pier. Jimmy and Jacob pushed Marilyn to the end of the pier.

"You boys go and have a look at the upper observation platform. I'll just sit here and think of Jeremy for a while if that's OK?" They agreed and said they would be back in thirty minutes.

"Lovely" she murmured. "Plenty of time."

She watched them go up the stairs and realised that where she was parked she was out of direct sight of them and everyone else. She sat for a few minutes in her wheelchair enjoying the breeze coming off the sea onto the pier. She had been placed so that when she reached into her pocket for another pebble, no one saw the resulting dust spill out of her hand onto the wooden pier and into the sea below. She waited for the breeze to get stronger and her pebble crumbled in her hand concealed within the pocket. This time the dust blew up and away from her heading towards shore. The next pebble crumbled but she didn't remove it from her pocket as she saw Jacob and Jimmy coming back down the stairs towards her.

"Could you push me to the disabled ladies' room, please?" she asked as they came back towards her.

"Course," said Jacob and they turned her wheelchair round and headed inside. Jacob pushed her into the toilet and she locked the door. As she had hoped, the floor was covered in sand from the beach. It looked like visitors had used the disabled loo as a private lockable changing area. She used the facilities but before opening the door again she scattered the remaining dust around on the floor and wheeled back and forth so it blended with the sand. Perfect she thought, as the dust dries in the warm room it would activate and become part of anyone who came into this room. Tourists and visitors from all around the country and possibly the world. The voice concurred inside her head.

...*your part was now done....your life can now restart....*

Marilyn smiled at Jacob and Jimmy as she came out of the toilet. They had come back with ice cream. "What a lovely end to another lovely day." She smiled at them both. They sat down on a bench with Marilyn parked beside them talking about the pier and the tourists all around them.

* * *

Joshua's turn came a few weeks later. He had planned to spread the dust at an international conference centre he was familiar with. 'Gamefestlive' was an event Joshua had gone to each year before COVID stopped these sorts of events. Now that vaccinations and restrictions were being lifted, #Gamefestlive was now trending on social media feeds, and Joshua planned to be there as a visitor, not a participant.

Sarah Keen had tried to persuade him to attend as one of the expert gamers there, but both Dave and Joshua had refused. Both of them knew this event could turn into a nightmare as any visitors and the media knew Joshua was one of the #sixaliveagain.

This new hashtag had gained ground after the video footage on Simon Kendal's channel replacing #sixnotdead as a more accurate tag of their current state. Joshua was not prepared to be recognised at the event so he asked Sarah Keen to get in touch with the film crew to see if any of them wanted a job making him look nothing like himself. Sarah found one of the runners also did stage makeup so it was arranged that they would come by the granny flat the day of the event and bring along a wig and accessories to enable Joshua to blend in without being recognised. On Saturday morning the door bell of the granny flat rang and Joshua went to the door. He was dressed and ready to go as he knew that this process would take a while.

On the step was a young man who said, "Hi," as Joshua opened the door. "I'm Lee, your make up man!" He smiled and didn't appear to recognise Joshua from the car park accident.

"Hi, come in," replied Joshua opening the door to let Lee in the apartment. Lee followed Joshua into the living room where a chair had been set up in preparation for the transformation. Dave was watching the news channel as they came into the room.

"Hi," said Lee smiling at Dave. Dave nodded and went out into the kitchen beckoning Joshua towards him

"Is this a good idea, Joshua?" Dave asked worriedly "What if you are recognised?"

"Sarah's coming with me, it will be fine," replied Joshua. "Anyway, she said that this guy can make me look so different even you wouldn't recognise your own child!" Dave nodded and walked out with Joshua to see Lee setting up his kit. He had a large case full of stage makeup, wigs, false teeth sets and other equipment and was eager to begin.

After one hour Dave had to agree with Lee, Joshua didn't look anything like himself and if Dave had passed Joshua in a corridor he would not have recognised his child. Only his eyes had remained their same colour, a vivid blue. Joshua's blond hair had been disguised with a wig of lanky greasy looking hair, and a bandanna covering it. Lee had also added a fake goatee beard which had made Joshua sneeze as it was being applied. Lee had also brought some baggy dungarees and a oversized tee shirt promoting some seventies band which added to the effect. Sarah had come in just as Lee was packing his kit up. She stood and admired Lee's work.

"Very good indeed Lee, excellent job!" she declared. "You ready Joshua?"

"Just need the loo – sorry," said Joshua who dashed to the bathroom. He had hidden the bag of pebbles Samir had given him in one of the ornamental jars in the bathroom. He flushed the loo and fished the bag out of the jar, carefully replacing it back on the shelf. He stashed the bag in one of the many pockets of the dungarees and grabbed his rucksack before joining Sarah at the front door.

"Have a good time," Dave said gruffly as he hugged him "and if you get tired, tell Sarah and she will bring you home" He glared at Sarah for confirmation.

She nodded. "Your dad's right, maybe not a full day at the event?" Joshua nodded, but he had plans which were not being put off track.

* * *

Sarah drove to the event being held at a conference centre in Birmingham in under three hours. The traffic was clear most of the way up and as Joshua observed, Sarah exceeded the speed limit frequently. She did however drive very well, she was observant and didn't crash Joshua thought

...I wouldn't die but she might...

The voice assured him

...the job was nearly done....

As they arrived at the conference centre, Sarah drove around to the premiere parking bays. "Don't want my car pranged, and we don't need a bus to get to where the car is parked here, unlike that lot" she indicated a busload of passengers getting off a shuttle bus signed "Car park E & F" on its front. Joshua nodded and followed Sarah into the reception area. They handed over their bags and went through the security before coming out into a massive indoor arena filled with stands and noise.

...Perfect, loads of people here...

Joshua scanned around looking for the staging area. Over to the right at the back was an auditorium screened by barriers and curtains. From inside Joshua could hear someone on a microphone announcing

"In the next session, Marco Foster will be demonstrating his skills against a member of the audience." Sarah and Joshua went over to where the people outside were queuing up. She indicated to Joshua to follow her to the front. At the barrier were two security men checking each person's ticket for access codes to get into the meet and greets.

"Hi Sam, Hi Merlin!" Sarah greeted both men who blushed. "Any chance me and the kid could slip in?"

The taller of the two lifted the gate and Sarah and Joshua slipped through to much moaning from the people still to be checked. Sarah looked over her shoulder and blew Sam and Merlin each a kiss, which made them blush even harder.

"Would you let me through for free if I blew you a kiss?" asked a spotty kid in an agitated voice

"Back of the line sir," said Merlin who grasped the kid's arm and propelled him back. The rest of the queue quietened down and waited for their turn. As Sarah and Joshua came into the seated area the lights were up on the stage. Sarah walked around to the centre of the seating and plonked herself down on one of the chairs. She patted the one beside her, but Joshua walked back to the last row and sat down where he could get a better view. Sarah nodded and turned back to the stage plucking out her mobile phone to see what messages she had received.

...this is good...wait until the lights go down...

Joshua sat waiting for the show to begin. Ten minutes later a presenter came out on stage "Good afternoon everyone. The show is about to begin. Can we have a member of the audience up to test their skills against Marco?"

Multiple hands reached out into the air, and the presenter chose a small spotty teenager who looked like he might be sick. The presenter escorted the teenager up to one side of the stage where a stagehand took some details from him.

From the other side of the stage came Marco Foster. Joshua knew who he was, Marco had been gaming online and hosting his own channel since the age of twelve. He was now nineteen, two years older than Joshua and over twenty places ahead of him on the ratings. Marco had made over five million pounds in sponsorship since he had started, and his management team were sitting in the front row watching their valuable asset perform.

As the lights went down in the seating area Joshua slipped the packet out of his pocket and into the front pocket of the dungarees. As he held it in his hands he felt the pebbles crumble within the bag into a fine dust. The presenter brought out the spotty kid who shielded his eyes from the glare of the lights trained on him, causing some of the audience to break out laughing. The presenter ushered the teenager to the front

"And what's your name?" he asked.

"Thomas" replied the teenager in a squeaky voice breaking sort of tone. That generated more laughter from the back near to where Joshua was sitting.

...them...those ones...they won't live much longer...

Joshua carefully opened the bag and took out a small handful of the dust. As he was above where the laughter was coming from he could pinpoint the group responsible. He lifted his hand and felt the breeze coming from the curtains behind him. As he released his hand, the dust swam up and then down directly onto the group who were giggling again as the presenter was asking the teenager basic questions about his favourite console and game.

No one sitting near them noticed the dust. The curtains surrounding the event had been in storage since before the first lockdown and hadn't been washed since. Quite a few people sitting down had been sprinkled with dust as the curtains had moved in the breeze from an open fire exit nearby. Joshua relaxed and watched the show. As predicted Marco had beaten the teenager but he had been worried for a while. Joshua could feel his anxiety

...this one is a good one...I didn't want to do this, I told them so...

Joshua felt this thought and knew it had come from Marco. He assumed that Marco was thinking about his management team.

...can I read minds now...

The voice replied

...No, but you can feel thoughts sometimes...

Joshua felt the voice was telling him the truth. He relaxed and watched the rest of the show and enjoyed it. Sarah came and found him afterwards and they went back into the arena to see what new games were about to be released. Sarah watched Joshua as they went around.

...Was a shame he had refused an expert slot on the stage...he could have beaten Marco easily...

Joshua smiled at Sarah. He had heard that one too. He knew she was right but he also knew if he had been on stage he would have heard Marco's plan in his head and could have offset any tactics he would have tried.

...Not cheating...but not fair either...

About halfway around the arena, they came across a cafe area. Joshua pleaded for a rest, and Sarah knew she needed a cigarette. Luckily there was both - a smoking area just to one side of the cafe and a place for Joshua to sit with a soft drink and a large sticky bun. Sarah got the food and her coffee and left them with Joshua whilst she went outside for the cigarette she had promised herself for the last hour. As she stood there she spotted Marco's manager standing by the wall. She went over to him.

"Hi Kelvin, long time no see!" Kelvin looked up.

"Hi Sarah, surprised to see you here. Heard your client died?"

Sarah gritted her teeth and smiled broadly back at Kelvin. "No Joshua is still alive. Haven't you heard he's one of the #sixaliveagain? Can't buy that publicity!" she added. "Unfortunately he wasn't able to come today. His dad wanted him to rest before he gets back on his channel next month."

"So who are you with today then?" asked Kelvin pointing back at the seating area where Joshua was demolishing his bun.

"Oh, that's just one of my film crew" Sarah nodded over at Joshua. "As the star couldn't come it seemed a shame to have a ticket going spare, so I put the names in the hat and lucky Adam was the winner" Kelvin nodded again. Sarah finished her cigarette and sauntered back over to Joshua.

"If Marco's manager comes over your name is Adam!" she hissed out of the corner of her mouth. Kelvin however finished his cigarette and just as he came back in, his mobile trilled urgently, and he fished it out of his pocket and answered.

"Looks like I'm safe" commented Joshua who had finished his bun. "Got sticky paws!" he said holding up his hands which were indeed covered with icing. "Just going for a pee, and a hand wash," he said as he stood up.

"Men's is over there" pointed Sarah. "I'll wait here for you" Joshua nodded and walked off.

...men's room...in a cubicle....that one....

Joshua walked over to the men's loos and walked into the last cubicle on the right. A line of men was at the urinals but Joshua needed a bit of privacy for this next step. He dropped his dungarees down to his feet and sat down. After urinating he fished out the plastic bag which was about half filled with dust. He lifted it to the light and saw it sparkle. He lifted the bag up and opened it. The cubicle he had chosen was deliberate. Above his head was an air vent leading to the air conditioning for the arena. In the cubicle even standing up no one could see Joshua tip up the bag, and watch as the dust was sucked up into the vent above him. He shook the bag to make sure all of the dust was gone, then dropped the bag back into his front pocket and did up his dungarees. He exited the loo, washed his hands, then went back out to where Sarah was finishing her coffee.

"Good to go?" she asked. "Yep, all good, clean paws" he replied showing her his hands. She smiled as they continued around the venue. Joshua smiled

...Your job is done...your life can begin again now...

Above their heads within the air conditioning system, the dust swirled and sparkled as it was driven by the fans surrounding the venue. No one noticed as sparkles descended around the venue onto notice boards, tables, speakers, and onto the heads of those walking below.

* * *

Jed and Kitty boarded the train to London the following week. Jed had surprised Kitty with the tickets as they were sat on the brown sofa after another long day. Kitty had been having coffee with Laura Jed's old nurse in one of the city cafes earlier. Jed was glad that Kitty had some support but he was also glad that she was still with him.

"How do you fancy a couple of nights in London?" Jed had announced as they sat on the sofa cuddling.

Kitty sat up straight. "London?" she queried.

"Yes, thought that we should have a couple of nights, seeing the sights. I wanted to go to London to see all the sights we missed but they kept bringing me back to that hell hole. I want to see what I missed., and us living in London, no one who lives there goes to see the Tower of London, unless they had relatives visiting."

Kitty patted his arm. "No drugs though - right?" She looked worried.

"No drugs, I'm clean, honest. Anyway, the drugs scene has got a bit frantic now Mr C is dead. The Russians are trying to muscle in, and I don't want to be near any of that!" Jed sat back and Kitty leaned against his chest. She took the tickets from him.

"A nice clean B&B near the sights, few tourist places, what do you say?"

She kissed him and leaned back again. "That would be lovely," she agreed. Jed smiled.

* * *

The following day they left the flat, with a small rucksack each. The neighbour on the top floor Professor Andrews had agreed to loan them each one. He had several as he would often be travelling around the world giving lectures. Kitty had been delighted to meet the Professor. After chatting over their respective mailboxes, Kitty had been invited to tea with the Professor who was now in his eighties. Jed hadn't minded. He knew that Kitty was lonely and he liked that she had started to make proper friends.

Jed and Kitty caught the first train after the rush hour and two hours later they were standing on the Paddington station steps getting their bearings. Jed had an underground train map in his hand.

"The B&B is just off the Waterloo station, so we need to go here," Jed pointed at the Hammersmith and City line "Paddington straight through to Waterloo. The B&B is about five minutes walk from there." Kitty nodded and held his hand as he directed them through the maze of commuters and tourists. Jed thought

...*She was scared*...

He held her hand tightly and smiled as they boarded the first of the trains they would need.

...*but not with me to protect her*...

The B&B was indeed clean and tidy and run by a Scottish lady whose accent was difficult to understand. They managed and after being shown the facilities they dumped their rucksacks in the room and went out to find food. After a few minutes walk they ended up in a quiet builders cafe around the corner from a massive building site. All the other customers wore high vis waistcoats and were drinking large mugs of stewed tea and eating huge cooked breakfasts despite it being lunchtime. Jed and Kitty sat down at a table next to the window.

Jed watched Kitty smile as she looked at the menu. "I think a cooked breakfast sounds nice," she commented. Jed went up to the counter and ordered two breakfasts with tea, he paid and came back to the table and said.

"Just gotta pee, be right back" She smiled and he went back to the counter "Have you got a customer loo?"

The girl manning the counter pointed to the door behind her on the right.

"Thanks," Jed said and he went into the loo. It smelt like one of the builders had been in here before him. It stank. He sat down on the loo and pulled one of the pebbles out of his pocket. He held it in his hand and watched it crumble into dust. He tipped up his hand and the dust fell out onto the floor. He sprinkled it around the cistern and next to the washbasin. As the dust dropped he heard the voice say

...nearly done...somewhere next ... busy...more people...

Jed nodded and washed his hands. He came out of the loo and bumped into the girl who had directed him to the toilet. She wrinkled her nose.

"Not me love, only had a pee" as he went back to the table where another girl was placing two large plates of cooked breakfast on the table. Once she had added two piping hot mugs of tea, Jed sat down and they both proceeded to eat.

Jed and Kitty started to plan their trip. Kitty had never visited the famous landmarks and she wanted to see everything. They planned their visits to see the bridges, the Tower of London, and at Kitty's request the National Gallery.

Kitty had developed a love of art at school but as she had descended into drugs living in Exeter her thoughts had been only of getting the next high. Now they were both clean, Kitty wanted to be inspired by the masters to start making her own art again. After finishing their huge breakfasts and tea, Jed and Kitty went back to the tube and started their tour.

They took the Jubilee Line to Stratford and got off at Tower Bridge station walking towards the iconic bridge. Kitty clapped her hands as they walked across the bridge towards the Tower of London. They saw the ravens and the Yeomen as they walked around the site and listened in on an elderly lady who was escorting a group of Americans around the site. They got close enough to hear her talk to the group but not so close as to cause suspicion that they were trying to get a free tour.

Jed excused himself again when he spotted the gents loos citing the large mug of tea being responsible for his weak bladder. Kitty smiled as she waited for him on a bench outside. Jed went into one of the cubicles and urinated. He was going to have to be careful not to attract Kitty's suspicions. He took out another pebble and watched it crumble in his hands. He scattered some inside the cubicle and as he exited he saw he was alone, so scattered the rest around the dryers on the wall. The hot air flow would move the dust around so it could rest and

...*infect?*...

The thought came to him.

...*What they were doing was helping the dust infect other people?*...

The voice replied

...*Helping them live when they are about to die*...

...*but what if they don't die?*...

he thought

...*Then we wait until they do*...

it replied. He calmed to hear the voice and went back outside to join Kitty who was still sitting on the bench now watching the ravens strut across the grass. As he came back to join her, she stood and hugged him.

"Tea all now gone?" she asked mischievously. "Old man with teeny tiny little bladder?" she continued.

"Yes I am an old man," replied Jed. "Now what about some culture woman!" She smiled as they made their way to the most famous art gallery in London. They caught the District Line to Embankment then walked to the steps of the Gallery which borders Trafalgar Square. They sat looking at Nelson on his column and admired the lions and other statues in the Square. It was busy with tourists taking selfies and pickpockets waiting for their opportunity to snatch a bag or two without being picked up by the police patrolling the area.

Jed and Kitty walked up the stairs into the Gallery and bought a guidebook and walk in tickets to view the free exhibits. Jed held Kitty's hand as she walked up to each of the paintings and just stared at them.

...she's drinking them in... Just keeping them in her mind for when she wants to look at them again...

Jed felt Kitty's joy in his brain. He knew he could feel what she was feeling now and he bathed in her joy and delight. As they walked around Jed too began to feel joy. He'd never been one for pictures. His education was intermittent and not something he had been proud of. He'd survived, that was all he wanted, but now the drugs had cleared from his brain, he realised that he did like the pictures.

...All of life is here.. he thought...the sad, the bad, the rich and poor...

Jed realised he wanted to know more. They walked to the gift shop and bought a lavishly coloured book about the paintings in the gallery. It would be the first of many purchases.

As they were waiting to pay Jed held the final pebble and carefully dropped the dust alongside him. No one noticed anything peculiar. The security guard on the exit was more interested in making sure people didn't steal any of the gift shop stock. As they exited the gallery Jed heard

...Your job is done...your life can begin again now...

Jed smiled and held Kitty's hand as she clutched the bag containing the book. They walked off following the crowd of commuters heading for the tube.

* * *

Samir registered on a veterinary degree course in Manchester that summer. Tamir came along with him to the open days and after speaking to one of the lecturers and providing his qualifications he became one of the youngest students on the four year course starting in the autumn. He was delighted to hear that there would be regular placements with surgeries in the local area for work experience, and with Tamir's apartment being close to campus Samir decided it would be better for him to stay there rather than going into halls.

Tamir was delighted that his cousin would finally be able to do the job he would love. Tamir's neighbours had two small cats who became firm friends with Samir and the love he gave them was obvious to everyone except his father. Tamir and Samir settled into a regular routine, Tamir was delighted to have Samir around for company, and Samir was glad to have a big brother in Tamir.

Samir hadn't forgotten about his promise to the dust. His first opportunity came on a visit to the freshers week in mid September. The hall it was being held in, was a frantic mix of social, sporting, and other activities which were open to the new student intake. Samir had decided that he needed to spread the dust in a location that would have a high amount of students coming through.

This place was perfect. Wide tall ceilings and many many students, staff, and visitors.

He walked around the hall slowly taking leaflets as they were being handed out. Three groups were of interest to him, volunteers for the local animal shelter, art appreciation, and Muslim students. He signed up for all three groups and got to meet his tutor and some of the students he was going to be studying with.

As he went around the hall again, he spotted a door marked toilets. He went inside, and into the fourth cubicle at the far end. Inside his jacket pocket, he had brought two of the pebbles. He took one out of them and placed it in his palm. As he watched the pebble vibrated violently and crumbled into dust, which he placed back into his pocket. He repeated the same action with the second pebble.

As he left the toilets with two crumbled pebbles in his pocket, he saw that the hall was even more crowded than before. He walked around slowly and carefully plucked a small handful of dust every so often out of his pocket, dropping it discreetly on the floor. No one noticed as the hall was packed with new students, and they were more interested in the groups and clubs on offer than what Samir was doing

...That is good, your work is nearly done...one more pebble...

Samir smiled as he left the building. He was going to really enjoy being a student again.

* * *

Three days later, Samir met up with Tamir for a curry in the centre of Manchester. Tamir had been working a long shift pattern and he wanted to catch up with his cousin and all he had been doing. Tamir chose his favourite restaurant which was located in the Rusholme area of South Manchester which was better known as the Curry Mile.

Samir had caught a bus from the apartment to stroll around the area. He loved living in Manchester, loved the buzz of the city. He walked slowly down the main road, looking at the window displays. As he walked he clutched the final pebble in his hand. He felt it crumble and he then withdrew his hand with dust inside it. Sprinkling it carefully as he walked, he realised that no one noticed him. He was just another customer of the area. After a mile, he reached the restaurant, and he saw Tamir inside talking to the staff. He walked into a delicious mix of spice and scents of curries. Tamir came over and hugged him.

"You look bushed, cousin," stated Samir.

"Been a hard set of shifts, but I am now off until Monday. After this meal I intend to sleep for a whole day," admitted Tamir. "Come and meet my friend Mohamed - his family has run this place for thirty years."

Samir shyly smiled at the tall dark man standing in front of him

"Welcome to my family restaurant, Samir. Tamir tells me you want a great Manchester curry - well this is the very best of these."

They were escorted to a table at the back of the restaurant, and Mohamed was true to his word. The food was great, and Samir made Mohamed laugh when he said

"This is better than my mother's." Tamir also laughed and said, "Don't let my auntie hear you say that cousin! but it's true." During the meal, Samir managed to drop more dust under the table, and as they were leaving Samir asked where the gents were. He was directed to a door at the very back of the restaurant. Inside was a single toilet. Samir dropped the remaining dust on the floor and under the hand dryer.

...your job is done...your life can begin again now...

The voice calmed him as he left the toilet, and as he walked across to his new family he smiled brightly. Life was going to be very good for him now, and all because of Matty Bartlett. Samir smiled. He wondered how Matty was getting on in prison on remand

* * *

Matty Bartlett had been remanded into custody and was currently at the bottom of a very long chain of command in the general wing of the only prison taking remand prisoners. All of the UK's prisons were massively overcrowded due to COVID preventing prisoners from going through trial and onto their sentences or freedom, which made for conflict over minor issues.

Matty had made the error of thinking he was a hard man, and within six hours he realised that his only hope was to become one of the real hard men's lackeys. The prisoner in question was an enemy of Mr C, his name was Marlow Kumarin. Mr C had fed the drug squad information on Marlow's network, and he was currently serving thirty years for drug distribution.

Matty was currently cleaning out the most disgusting lavatory in history. He had been warned not to gag but he was in fear of passing out from shock or lack of oxygen. He excused himself frequently for a gasp of fresh air outside the cell, which caused ripples of laughter from Marlow and his friends. After many minutes of hell, he had completed the task and stood dripping with sweat and stains on his clothes he didn't want to think about.

"Very good, my dear boy," Marlow said from his bunk. "Michas had a bad tummy yesterday. I didn't think anyone could get that toilet clean again" He indicated the biggest of the thugs surrounding the doorway. "Michas - do you need the toilet again?"

The thug nodded and Marlow ushered Matty out of the door. "Better not go too far, You'll be needed again in a bit" Matty gulped then walked down the stairs to his cell. He really hated Samir now.

Two hundred miles away Samir smiled broadly. He could hear Matty's howls of anguish inside his head.

* * *

Brian had confirmed to Catherine and Katie the week before that he wanted to join them for the Open Day at the University. Catherine had reacted with concern when Brian had suggested it, though as she had observed, Brian's COPD seemed to be stabilising. Brian appealed to her compassion, to let him see where Katie was going to be living for the next few years. Brian knew she was right, his COPD was slowly getting better, very slowly. He still needed the oxygen especially at night, but he was feeling fitter than he had done for years.

Mrs Bateman had tried to block the visit, but Catherine had been insistent that her father wasn't a prisoner in this home, and refusing the opportunity for him to see where his granddaughter was going to be studying would result in the media being informed.

Catherine had no intention of letting the media into her life any more than it was already, but the threat worked, and Brian was supplied with a small oxygen tank and given leave for three days. Catherine was asked to sign a waiver that Brian was leaving and she would not be able to sue the home if he died on the trip. Catherine signed with a flourish as did Brian and they both smiled at Mrs Bateman as Brian handed the waiver back.

...If he dies on the trip, Magdeline and the others would come back to work...

Mrs Bateman was unsettled by Brian's presence and as she looked at him, he smiled even more broadly.

...Did I say that out loud, does he know what I think of him?...

Brian did know what she was thinking. This was a gift of the dust, which in him was far more advanced than the others. Perhaps it was his age, and experience of being able to read people, but Brian knew that the others were also experiencing glimpses of people's thoughts.

...This is a lot of fun...

* * *

Catherine drove Brian and Katie down for the Open Weekend the following day. She had arranged for them to stay in one of the city hotels, and after parking her car, and checking in, Brian asked if he could have a short rest before they went out to eat. Katie and Catherine made Brian comfortable with his oxygen in his room, which was adjacent to theirs.

Katie had been thrilled when Catherine had confirmed Brian was coming along but warned her not to overexcite her granddad and not be too disappointed if he couldn't make the trip after all. Katie had been sent a bundle of information from the University and had also researched several nursing courses online. Catherine and Katie spread out the information on one of the beds in their room.

"This one is for three years, but this one" Katie pointed to a colourful leaflet " is for four years but one of those years is on placement throughout the hospital network." Catherine and Katie had already established that Katie could receive full funding for the course she wanted to do. A lack of nurses in the NHS had meant funding options were generous, although Catherine would have to contribute towards the costs. Brian lay on his bed listening to the chatter, and hearing the thoughts of his child and grandchild. As he dozed off, he knew he would be able to help as well.

* * *

The following day, Catherine, Katie, and Brian got out of the taxi in front of the Hall hosting the Open Weekend at the University in Bournemouth. The lobby area and halls were packed with people, Brian was in his wheelchair with his oxygen bottle stashed underneath, but he felt great. As they moved around the room, Brian heard many thoughts from those students and parents around him but he had learned to tune them down like turning down the volume on his TV.

Katie and Catherine were delighted to learn that the course they had preferred would accept Katie with the grades she had been predicted to get. Brian sat to one side of the stall they were standing at. He smiled at Katie and Catherine and could hear their joy at the news. After a few minutes, Katie came over.

"Are you OK, Granddad?"

"Yes my love, but could you push me over to that disabled loo over there?"

Katie grasped the wheelchair handles and propelled Brian over to the toilet. She opened the door and wheeled him inside.

"No need to wait, love, I can manage."

"Are you sure?" Katie asked concerned.

"Yes I am more stable on my feet these days, but stay outside if that's OK?"

"Course," said Katie with a smile as she shut the door. Brian used the toilet, then sat back down on the wheelchair. He took out his jacket which had been tucked underneath the oxygen bottle. He quickly put the jacket on and felt the pebbles inside the plastic bag Samir had given him. He held the bag for a few seconds, feeling the pebbles crumble inside the bag. He slipped the bag back into his pocket and wheeled himself back to the door.

"I'm ready!" he said, and Katie opened the door, and wheeled him back to where Catherine was talking to the tutors. She turned around as they came back

"Bladder emergency!" said Brian with a smile "All sorted now." Katie pushed Brian back to where he had been before. "You leave me here chickie and go and speak to your tutors."

"Are you sure, Granddad?" Katie asked. "Will you be OK?"

"Yes, now my bladder is sorted." He waved her back to Catherine and then sat watching the room. No one really noticed him, sat there. After a few minutes, he carefully reached into his pocket and opened the bag. He stuck his hand into the bag and felt the crumbly dust vibrate. He took a small amount out and leaning his arm down, he released it on the carpet. He'd observed the carpet was a mud grey colour and seemed to have been chosen for high wear and tear.

Behind him was an electric fan that was blowing warm air over the room. As he dropped the dust, it swirled and sparkled in the carpet, then started to be lifted by the fan.

No one noticed him sitting in the corner in his wheelchair. He heard their thoughts

...He's a bit old to be at University...

...Is that one of our tutors??!..

Brian smiled and continued to reach into his pocket and sprinkle more dust around. After a few more minutes Catherine and Katie were done. Catherine held a map in her hand

"Did you want to see the accommodation block, Dad?" The tutor said they are open for visits as well."

"Yes please!" said Brian patting Katie's hand "Are you happy, chickie?"

She smiled and said "Much better having you here to see where I am going to be living" she confirmed.

She turned Brian's chair around and they headed off following Catherine to the other side of the grounds. Katie and Brian took the disabled lift next to the stairs and they made their way down a corridor of bright and airy rooms.

Each was decorated in bright colours and several had already been claimed by overseas students who were already enrolled. Katie pushed Brian down to a large open communal kitchen area where more students were hunched over their laptops. Katie beamed as she looked around the room. One of the students with a badge marked 'Alison - student services' came over to them and asked

"Hello, are you a new student this coming year?" to Katie. She nodded. "Right well you have seen the rooms, this is the kitchen and study area. There are three rooms like this in the block so if one is busy you can go to any of the others. What are you going to be studying?"

"Nursing," replied Katie shyly

"Oh great, Sam here," she indicated a dark-haired, girl "is doing the same course as you" Sam looked up as she heard her name and waved at the group. "We have a few Nursing students in this block. It's accidental but useful if you want to get into a study group" Alison continued. "And these are your family?"

Catherine came over and introduced herself and Brian. Brian smiled apologetically and said, "Do you have a disabled loo here?"

Alison pointed to the other end of the room. "Down that corridor on the left."

Katie pointed Brian's wheelchair towards the loo and opened the door for him. "Right outside, Grandad," she confirmed as she closed the door. Brian nodded as the door closed and he carefully locked the door. He looked up into the ceiling of the toilet room. In one corner was an air conditioning vent. He pushed himself over towards it and felt the air flowing towards the vent.

..Perfect, just what I needed...

Brian took out the plastic bag which was still half full of crumbled dust. He opened the bag and could feel the dust start to vibrate inside the bag. He lifted the bag upwards and felt the dust start to lift in the currents of air under the vent. As he watched the dust sparkled and shone and rose upwards in visible currents. After a few seconds, the bag was empty.

...Your job is done...your life can begin again now...

Brian smiled. The voice was right, he would have a great life now, he felt better than he had done for a long while. He tucked the bag back into his pocket and carefully unlocked the door. He opened it slightly and was glad to see Katie talking to the girl named Sam just down the corridor. He coughed and Katie blushed and came running to help him out of the toilet.

"Made a friend, chickie?"

Katie nodded. "Sam's from just down the coast from Exeter."

Brian patted her hand. "This has been lovely, Katie. This is a great place for you to study at. I'm so glad that I was able to come along." Katie smiled as she wheeled Brian back to the kitchen area where Catherine was talking to Alison. Catherine glanced over at her dad

...He looks brighter, perhaps it's good for him to get out after all?...

Katie pushes Brian back to where Catherine and Alison still are chatting.

...This trip has been good for all of us...

Catherine thinks. They say goodbye to Alison and make their way back to the road where a taxi rank was situated.

"This has been a very good trip I would say," says Brian as they help him into the taxi. "Yes," agreed Catherine "it really has."

* * *

23

Second Outbreak.

The pretty and scenic town of Ambleside had welcomed visitors and residents since the late 1650s. Ambleside's name is derived from the Old Norse "Á-mel-sǽtr" which literally translates as "river – sandbank – summer pasture." Ambleside sits at the north end of the biggest lake in the area - Lake Windermere. In the stifling heat of a warm July day, the tourists and locals were enjoying the cool waters and forest walks in the area. Windermere is one mile wide, 10.5 miles long, and 220 feet deep.

On the shoreline, one group was making plans to enjoy the lake. Since lockdown restrictions had eased, more tourists had come back to the area, including a hen party from Manchester. The hen's consisted of chief hen Heather, super organized, and a force to be reckoned with, the bride to be - Amy who worked with Heather in a local government office, and Amy's younger and plainer sister Maggie who worked as a teacher in a primary school in Salford.

The other three members of the party had reluctantly cancelled after being pinged at a local nightclub the weekend before and had been forced to self isolate. Heather was tall and slim and didn't look her age which was thirty two. She had a shock of red hair which refused to behave and she normally wore it in a severe bun for her job.

Amy was blonde, aged twenty six, and was a Finance Officer for the local council. She had been working from home as had all of her colleagues including Heather since the first lockdown, but this was her chance to get out of Manchester and make good memories. Maggie, as a key worker hadn't had the opportunity to "work-from-home" as her sister and Heather had.

During the whole of the last sixteen months, she had been forced to be at school to manage the remote and bubble learning of year 8 pupils. Her students were a great bunch but most of them struggled to access online learning so the headmistress had decided to bubble the students into class groups. Unfortunately, a lot of the students had parents who had been exposed to COVID and as a result, her class groups had got behind as they had been forced back home to isolate themselves.

...Heather had been a nightmare in being allowed to organize the hen party, in my humble opinion. Give someone who already thinks she is in charge, the official ability to be in charge - horrific....

Amy had pleaded with Maggie to "go along with it" so Maggie had reluctantly agreed and currently sat on the shoreline trying to zip up a wet suit with limited success. Amy's plan for the hen weekend involved a lot of water and not the frozen sort you eventually dilute a nice cocktail with, but actual water sports.

Amy's particular joy it seemed was paddleboarding, a uniquely complex method of standing up on a type of surfboard and keeping your balance whilst propelling yourself across the water. Heather had tried this sport in Cyprus a couple of years ago, and it seemed she had been quite good at it. This meant that a majority out of the three in the group had decided that this was a great way to start off the weekend. Unfortunately, Maggie wasn't keen on the water except perhaps looking at it and paddling in a safe and warm swimming pool with a cocktail on a nearby bar to look forward to. She could swim, but didn't really like cold water.

She had realized that the heat of the shoreline wouldn't transfer into the deep water of the lake and if she went in, it would be cold. She had asked for a wet suit to go over her one piece swimming costume, which had made Heather snigger.

...Heather was clad in teeny tiny shorts and a bikini top and looked amazing for her age. Amy too looked great in her swimming costume, she had been hitting the gym since her fiance Johnny had proposed on New Year's Eve at the local club...

Heather had been unhappy with the instructor who had insisted that they all wear life jackets, as the bright orange clashed with her hair. However, she had been told that if they didn't wear the jackets they couldn't rent the paddle-boards. The instructor couldn't be persuaded so here they all were, sitting on the boards in the dirt by the lake getting some instructions before they set off. They all wore hired rubber-soled water shoes for extra grip on the boards.

Maggie was the only one who was paying attention, as she really didn't feel safe on the board. She was reassured by the life jacket, however. Over on the far side of the group, Heather was kicking her feet in the dirt in frustration as she was forced to listen to instructions she clearly thought she already knew. In the sunlight, small particles of dust floated up and sparkled as she kicked her feet up again and again.

* * *

Thirty minutes later they set off from the wooden pier. Maggie was petrified at first, but she began to relax, as the warm sun beat down on her suit. There was a light breeze and it helped to propel them all along. Maggie looked over at Amy who was grinning broadly.

"See sis, it's great isn't it?" Maggie nodded.

...If only the hen party had been her and Amy on their own. She wouldn't have made her feel like a freak. On the other side of her, Heather was easily propelling herself along using smooth strokes and keeping her balance. She looked like she belongs on the water like some sort of Norse Goddess, the sunlight sparkling on her wet skin....

Maggie turned back to Amy, she wasn't going to let Heather upset her. Her older sister was getting married, and she wanted her to have an amazing time. Heather continued to propel herself along easily.

In the distance, a large motorboat was coming around for another pass. A few minutes after it sped off, the wake waves started to come closer to the group. Amy shouted a warning to the others, she had seen this before. Amy crouched down on the board and held onto the sides, as the wake wave came closer. Maggie followed her lead and crouched on her board as well.

Looking over at Heather, Maggie realized that Heather had taken off her life jacket and it was hooked onto the white and blue Alpha flag at the back of her board, and she had not seen the wake coming closer.

As the wake hit Heather's board she stumbled and fell into the water, hitting her head on the board as she went in. Amy immediately took off her own jacket and dived in the water, her arms smoothly gliding through the water. Maggie knew that her sister was a good swimmer, and had done her lifeguarding course with the local swimming club a few years ago.

Amy swam to Heather's board but she wasn't floating in the water. Taking a deep breath Amy dived under the board looking for Heather. She surfaced a few feet away. Maggie looked around and saw a motorboat nearby - she waved frantically to them, and the boat swung around and came closer.

"What's happened?" asked the young man who was driving the motorboat.

"Our friend she got unbalanced by the wake from that boat over there. She hit her head hard and my sister is looking for her."

"I'm Jack, I'll call for help."

Maggie pointed to where Amy had surfaced again. Amy took a deep breath and went back down. Thomas took out his radio and called for help. As Amy surfaced again, she held the limp body of Heather around her shoulders. She swam over to the boat where Maggie was treading water.

"She's not breathing," said Amy with a gasp as she drags Heather across. Maggie pulled herself up into the boat and helps Jack with Heather's limp form. Amy drags herself up and starts CPR.

Heather is not breathing but Amy can hear a strong heartbeat. As Jack turns the boat around and heads back to shore calling for an ambulance to meet them at the dock, Amy continues to give rescue breaths to Heather who is not breathing. Maggie shivers sitting in the boat as her sister tries to bring Heather back. A few minutes later the dockmaster and the paddleboard instructor meet them at the dock. In the distance, Maggie can hear the wail of an ambulance.

Heather doesn't breathe, her heart beats strongly but she doesn't die.

* * *

About the Author

Janet lives in Oxfordshire UK, when she isn't writing, she enjoys knitting socks.

You can connect with me on:
- https://twitter.com/dustbooksauthor
- https://www.facebook.com/DustBooksAuthor

Also by Janet Humphrey

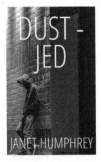

DUST - Jed

Jed was loved by his mum Clare even though they lived in squats and on the streets of Exeter in the United Kingdom. Their life was hard but when she died he was forced to grow up in a local church children's home. Bullied both at school and home, his life spiralled out of control despite the kindness of some to try and help him. His story, his life, and how he came to be a key part of the DUST.

DUST Book Two

Coming soon

The DUST has been deliberately spread by the original #sixnotdead. More people around the United Kingdom are infected, the world is not prepared for the outcome. Can the DUST be stopped before catastrophic events unfold.?

Would you like to read Book Two before publication? Apply to be a beta reader by contacting me via the Facebook link on the author page

Printed in Great Britain
by Amazon

16567358R00190